"Ahhh!" Hope's terrified cry split the twilight . . .

Something whizzed by her ear. A stone cracked the windshield of the car behind her. Suddenly she was running, her heart pounding in her ears, horror racing through her body. Her legs seemed to be moving all by themselves. She took off into the trees, dodging bushes and fallen logs. Hope was running too hard even to turn around to glance behind her, was too afraid to see April's murderer chasing after her.

Keep going. Keep running, she told herself. *It's your only chance.*

As she sprinted between two rows of peach trees, another flat stone whipped by her, ricocheting off the trunk of a tall tree. Then a sharp pain shot through her entire body as a jagged rock tore her cheek. Hope stumbled and slammed into a huge root swelling out of the ground beneath her. She screamed in pain as she felt herself going down, falling, collapsing on the grass.

Hope reached up and touched her face, then looked down at her hand. It was covered in dark red blood.

Find out **Who Killed Peggy Sue?**
Read:

#1 *Dying to Win*
#2 *Cross Your Heart, Hope to Die*
#3 *If Looks Could Kill*
#4 *Jailbird*

Available from Puffin Books

Who Killed Peggy Sue?

Cross Your Heart, Hope to Die

Created by Eileen Goudge

PUFFIN BOOKS

PUFFIN BOOKS
Published by the Penguin Group
A division of Penguin Books USA Inc.,
375 Hudson Street, New York, New York 10014, U.S.A.
Penguin Books Ltd, 27 Wrights Lane, London W8 5TZ, England
Penguin Books Australia Ltd, Ringwood, Victoria, Australia
Penguin Books Canada Ltd, 10 Alcorn Avenue, Toronto, Ontario, Canada M4V 3B2
Penguin Books (N.Z.) Ltd, 182-190 Wairau Road, Auckland 10, New Zealand

Penguin Books Ltd, Registered Offices: Harmondsworth, Middlesex, England

First published in 1991 by Viking Penguin, a division of Penguin Books USA Inc.

3 5 7 9 10 8 6 4 2

Produced by Daniel Weiss Associates, Inc.
33 West 17th Street, New York, New York 10011
Copyright © 1991 Eileen Zuckerman and Daniel Weiss Associates, Inc.
Cover illustration copyright © 1991 Daniel Weiss Associates, Inc.
All rights reserved

Library of Congress Catalog Card Number: 91-52895
ISBN 0-14-034888-3
Printed in the United States of America
Set in Avanta

April Lovewell, 17, was student at Paradiso High School

Paradiso was shocked by the senseless Thursday night murder of April Constance Lovewell. The seventeen-year-old Paradiso High School student was found strangled to death in a school locker. Sheriff Rodriguez said that as of today, no suspects have been named and no motive has been determined for the killing.

April Lovewell was the daughter of Reverend Ward and Mrs. Sara Lovewell. She had recently been elected Queen of the Paradiso Peach Blossom Festival. She would have graduated from high school this June. According to friends and acquaintances of Ms. Lovewell, she was a gifted student of painting and dreamed of becoming a professional artist.

Services will be held on Monday at 10:30 A.M. at the Church of Christ. Interment will be in Paradiso Cemetery.

In lieu of flowers, the family of the deceased requests contributions to the church.

CHAPTER 1

"My baby! My little girl!" Sara Lovewell moaned, and Hope Hubbard actually felt a little sorry for her aunt Sara as she watched her cousin April's body being lowered into the fresh, raw hole in the earth.

The coffin hung in the grave from two leather straps, attached to pulleys by several feet of cord—not too different from the cord that had been used to squeeze April's last breath out of her. A worker in a faded green uniform slowly turned the crank.

Hope swallowed hard. She felt numb. It was so mechanical, like watching a demolition ball being raised on a crane to smack away at an old building, or listening to the whirring and clicking of machine parts as her computer booted up. She couldn't believe April was in that box in the ground. Was this it? No parting of the bright blue California sky overhead? No sudden rustling of the treetops around the Paradiso town cemetery as April was put in her final resting place? Not even a cloud marked Hope's cousin's departure or offered a fleeting moment of relief from the strong sun. Just a few words from a minister, the sobs of the crowd, and the squeaking of the pulley system as the coffin went into the ground.

Hope watched the worker throw the first shovel of dirt on April's grave. On the other side of the hole in the ground, Aunt Sara, April's mother, let out another moan of anguish. "April . . ."

Uncle Ward put a bony hand on his wife's shoulder, piously bowing his head. It should have been a gesture that came naturally to him, after a lifetime of leading his congregation from the pulpit, but his tight, thin face reflected the shock and disbelief caused by a death that was anything but natural.

For once, Hope's mother refrained from making a comment about her brother, putting aside her bitterness for her daughter's sake. Ward Lovewell and Leanne Hubbard hadn't been on speaking terms for almost seventeen years, ever since Hope's father had picked up and left. But Hope felt a mild sense of relief to see that tears shone in her mother's eyes anyway. Her mom had disapproved of Hope's friendship with April. "If you're not good enough for Ward and Sara, then their daughter isn't good enough for you," she had remarked about once a day. But April had been Leanne's niece, after all—tied to her by blood. And her murder was such a startling blow to everyone. As if in acknowledgment of their mutual loss, she slipped her hand in Hope's.

Around them, the crowd was starting to break up. People turned away from the grave site to wend their way through orderly rows of tombstones.

The sea of darkly clad mourners moved to the cemetery gate. Paradiso High was closed for the day. Hope and her mother had passed it on the way to the funeral service. No sign of life. Someone had, however, been by to raise the flag—just to half-mast. The stars and stripes wilted around the flagpole in a breezeless morning that was already warm.

A keening wail pierced the stifling air. Hope turned to see Penny Bolton, her face distorted by tormented sobs. For a moment, Hope felt disgusted. While April was alive, Penny had made it known—as often and as harshly as possible—that she had no use for April. Then Hope remembered Penny's infant sister, who had died in her sleep not long ago. Maybe Penny wasn't crying crocodile tears. Maybe she just couldn't take a second senseless death.

Hope's shoulders sagged as she turned away from

Penny. As far as she was concerned, one senseless death was more than anybody should have to bear.

Judging from the faces around her and the ones she had seen earlier at the memorial service, Hope suspected everyone else felt the same way. It seemed that all of Paradiso had turned out to say good-bye to April. Hope doubted that a single store was open in town, or that a single car was rolling down Old Town Road. People had loved April. That was why she had been chosen Peach Blossom Queen—nicknamed Pretty Peggy Sue for the 1950s theme of this year's Peach Blossom Festival. Everybody had loved her.

Well, everybody but one person. It seemed impossible that anyone would do such a horrible thing. April had been genuinely kind and caring. She was beautiful. She had never really believed it —she'd always worried over those extra few pounds and all her freckles. But people around her could see her beauty, and they knew she was the most talented artist at school. Why would anyone want to snuff out her life?

Hope felt a fresh stream of tears sting her eyes. April would never get to wear the Peach Blossom crown, never collect the college scholarship she'd won, nor have a chance at the Hollywood screen test that so many of the kids at school fantasized about. Poor April hadn't even had a chance to hear

the news that she had won Peach Blossom Queen.
And now it wouldn't make any difference to her.
Nothing would, ever again.

A picture surfaced in Hope's mind of her school
locker and April's arm, bluish and lifeless, dangling
from it. Then the rest of her body tumbling out as
Hope opened her locker door farther.

Hope bit back a cry and tried to push the gruesome image to the furthest corner of her mind. But
how could she?

Leanne Hubbard pulled Hope closer to her,
steering her away from April's grave.

"Come on, sweetheart," she said softly.

Hope took one more look over her shoulder at
the hole in the ground and at Aunt Sara and Uncle
Ward standing paralyzed behind it. She wished she
could run over to them and throw her arms around
them. They were April's family—as Hope was.
They had loved April as much as Hope did. But
Hope knew that her aunt and uncle would turn a
stiff shoulder to her embrace. Aunt Sara had
avoided meeting Hope's eyes across the grave site,
and Uncle Ward had given her a hard glance and
quickly looked away. Hope had seen a flash of re-
sentment in his eyes, as if he felt bitter that his
sister still had her daughter while he had lost his.

It was so unfair that the adults had extended
their poisonous family feud to April and Hope.

7

This tragedy should be a time for extra peace and sympathy, a time to reunite and to console one another. But Uncle Ward and Aunt Sara had made it clear they didn't feel that way.

People would be going over to Uncle Ward's church now, to sit with each other and cry and talk about their memories of April. Hope felt a trill of anger that she couldn't be there. She wanted to be there. She belonged there, with the people who had loved April best. Instead, she and her mother would go back to their little house—alone. Hope couldn't imagine how she was going to make it through the afternoon.

The people who had loved April best. That was it. Something had been bothering Hope as her eyes scanned the crowd, and now she knew what it was. Somebody was missing: Spike Navarrone, April's boyfriend. She had not seen him at the service or at the cemetery. Somehow, she would have noticed Spike or felt his presence. He had been April's boyfriend, and she had been April's best friend. It was an instant bond between them.

Spike had good reason to keep a low profile. He and April had kept their romance a secret from Uncle Ward and Aunt Sara, who would never have approved of Spike—a motorcycle-riding auto-shop student who lived in a trailer way beyond the wrong side of town—in a trillion years. Maybe he was just making himself scarce. Hope looked toward the fringes of the crowd, toward the back, even at the grave site, which gleamed like a fresh wound that had just painfully ripped open the skin of the earth.

No Spike. He wasn't there; Hope knew it. A dark thought entered her mind. What if Spike had stayed away from April's funeral because he had something else to hide?

No! Spike had loved April!

"C'mon, sweetie," Leanne Hubbard urged, misinterpreting Hope's fierce gaze, which had fixed on April's grave.

Closing her eyes, Hope sighed and turned away. "Mom, do you think we could maybe—I don't know—go for a walk or something?" she asked.

Leanne Hubbard gave Hope a sad smile. People said they looked alike, with the same fine features, dark hair and eyes against pale skin, and tall, reed-thin figures.

"Honey, we can do whatever you want to do," she said.

Hope and her mother headed arm in arm toward the main gate of the cemetery, following the direction of the numerous mourners.

"Hope!" someone behind them called.

Hope turned around to see Jess Gardner coming over. His lean swimmer's body was hidden under a dark suit, but he looked as handsome as ever, with his full lips, strong chin, and reddish-blond hair falling over his blue eyes. Jess was with Raven Cruz and Vaughn Cutter.

A fleeting ray of brightness broke through Hope's grief. "Hey, Jess. Hi," she said to Raven and Vaughn.

"How are you doing?" Jess asked.

"This must be worse for you than anyone else," Raven added.

Hope took in the concern on all three of their faces. "I'm all right. Thanks, guys." As her eyes met Jess's, a deep look of empathy passed between them. Jess had been there when Hope had found April's body. He had revived her when she'd fainted and held her close during that terrible, awful moment. Jess, too, was a victim of the grisly image that would haunt Hope forever.

Hope let her gaze drop from Jess's face. Until last week, she had thought she would give anything to get closer to him. Anything. But not this. Not in her worst nightmares had she dreamed it would be her cousin's life.

Raven reached out and gave Hope's hand a squeeze, her silver bracelets jangling softly and catching the sun. "Hey," she said. She held Hope's hand in hers for a moment.

Hope noticed that Raven's eyes were swollen and rimmed with red. She had been crying. Crying for

April, even though April had cost her the title of Pretty Peggy Sue. But now Raven managed a smile. Hope knew it was for her.

"You look really pretty, Raven," Hope said. Even in her somber navy dress, Raven had style. The dress ended above the knee and was slightly flared. A lace-trimmed, white handkerchief peeked out of the breast pocket, and she wore a very cool pair of blue suede ankle boots. Her hammered silver earrings matched her bracelets, and her jet black hair hung in a thick braid down her back.

Hope couldn't help thinking that April would have loved Raven's outfit. She had always admired Raven's flair for dressing—especially since Raven made all her own clothes.

It was typical of April, like their conversation the week before: "If I had to place a bet on that computer program you've dreamed up about who's going to win Peggy Sue," April had said to Hope, "I'd bet that Raven Cruz will whip up the most outrageous ball gown in the history of the Peach Blossom Festival."

While the other three Peach Blossom Queen hopefuls were squabbling with each other and feeding the Paradiso High gossip mill, April had stayed friends with all of them. Hope was sure that was why the festival Queen selection committee had decided to choose her. April had the kind of human goodness Uncle Ward only preached about.

Raven shrugged at Hope's compliment. "Thanks, Hope, but I don't feel pretty today," she said, her voice wavering a little.

"No one does," Vaughn added. As she let go of Hope's hand, Raven slipped her arm through Vaughn's. Was it official? Were they a couple now? They looked good together. Raven—dark and slender, with a style all her own. Vaughn—chisel featured and fair haired in a traditional but elegantly cut suit. "Hope, we're really sorry," he said.

Hope nodded. "You guys know my mom, don't you?" she asked.

"Yeah, hi, Mrs. Hubbard," they said, not precisely in unison.

"Hello, boys," Leanne Hubbard said to Jess and Vaughn. "Hi, Raven. How's your mother feeling? I saw her when she came in to see the doctor a few days ago." Hope's mother was a nurse.

"She's still in bed, but she wants to be up and back in the café soon," Raven said. Raven's family owned Rosa's, a tiny Mexican café not too far from Hope's house. Raven and all her brothers and sisters helped out there.

Hope and her friends and mother stood silently for a few moments. Nearby, people hugged and cried quietly. Hope sneaked another look at Jess.

12

He was so handsome. He caught her gaze and held it. She wanted to thank him for being there for her when she'd needed it, for staying calm despite his own fright, for soothing her panicked cries. Kids said Jess could fix anything. They meant in his father's auto repair shop. But Jess had helped keep Hope from breaking down completely as she'd stared at April's body on the hall floor.

"Well," said Raven. "We just wanted to see how you were doing, Hope."

"If there's anything you need . . ." Jess said.

"Yeah, we're here," Vaughn added.

Hope nodded. "Same," she told them. "See you at school."

Too weird. Tomorrow Hope would be going to classes at Paradiso High, just the way she always did. But there would be no April, sitting under her favorite tree, sketching. No April to share lunch and the latest Paradiso gossip with. There would be only grief and emptiness—and fear. Because April's killer was still out there, and it could be anyone. Even someone Hope thought was a friend. In fact, people were saying it *had* to be a "friend," because whoever left the body in Hope's locker either knew the combination or got it from April. Hope's combination was legendary at Paradiso High: 35-23-35, supposedly Lacey Pinkerton's measurements. Practically everybody at school, with the possible exception of Lacey, knew about it. But it wasn't the sort of thing anybody outside school would know.

Hope watched Jess go off with Raven and Vaughn. Were they April's friends? Boy, the heat must be getting to me, she thought, wiping her forehead with the back of her hand. Hot and sunny. Another typical day in Paradiso. Except that April Lovewell had just been buried. And there was a murderer on the loose.

CHAPTER 2

"Okay, okay, I'll be there in a minute." A single teardrop inched its way down Lacey Pinkerton's cheek. She was not looking forward to spending the rest of the day alone or, even worse, with her parents. "Why don't you wait for me in the limo with Daddy? I'll really be just a minute, Mother," she said, with a sharp emphasis on *Mother*.

Lacey knew that behind those jewel-rimmed extra-dark sunglasses, on the face that was an older version of her own, her mother's eyes showed nothing but dissatisfaction and anger. No one ever quite measured up to Mrs. Darla Pinkerton, Paradiso's first Peach Blossom Queen from who knew how long ago.

Pointing an unsteady finger at Lacey, she warned, "One minute and not a second more. I've got plans for this afternoon." And with that

15

ultimatum she turned and stormed off, not stopping even for a second to pay respect to April's family or friends.

Lacey had a good deal of experience dealing with Darla—or rather, not dealing. Darla was too wrapped up in herself to pay any attention to Lacey. Lacey had learned to treat her mother the same. Today would certainly be no different.

If anything, Lacey thought, today should be for me! After all, I'm grieving. As if my friend April being murdered by some cold-blooded maniac weren't enough. Meanwhile, here I am, the hottest, most popular girl in Paradiso and not only did I lose the Peach Blossom contest, I don't even have a boyfriend to hold on to. She couldn't remember the last time she had been single.

Lacey felt a flood of tears about to gush from her eyes. She reached into the front pocket of her long black mourning dress and pulled out a dazzling, hot pink silk handkerchief, which she used to dab the tears. She was sure all the Pinks would have liked to have worn a touch of something pink amid all that black to show that the Pinks cared too. But only Lacey had actually had the nerve to pull it off. Wiping her tears away, she made a conscious attempt to display the handkerchief, giving it a little wave before she tucked it back into her front pocket. She nonchalantly looked around to make sure her display had not gone unnoticed.

Today nothing would go unnoticed. The air, so filled with shock, with so much confusion and so little hope, made everyone in Paradiso ultra-sensitive. All the mourners seemed to be sneaking accusing looks at one another, as if their own neighbors had turned into murderers overnight.

The silk handkerchief was Lacey's magic wand. Within seconds she was surrounded by her ever-faithful court.

Renée Henderson, hand in hand with Doug Mattinsky, and Lacey's most faithful attendant, Penny Bolton, clinging heavily to boyfriend Hal Bemis, came to console Lacey.

"Once a Pink always a Pink, hey, Lacey?" Renée gave Lacey a big, strong hug. Sobbing, Renée held the hug for an extra moment. She shook uncontrollably as she leaned down and whispered into Lacey's ear, "I don't think I can handle it, Lacey. Really, I just can't handle this one. I'm gonna flip!"

Lacey held on to Renée. "Calm down, honey," she said in her definitive manner that everyone knew so well. "Listen to me." She pulled away and gave Renée an authoritative look. "Don't get hysterical. You're gonna pull yourself together. I promise. Listen to Lacey, just listen to Lacey. Okay?"

But Renée was over the edge. Her usually

17

gorgeous, gold-flecked hair was a disheveled mess. The sight of her, the tallest girl in school, trembling in the Paradiso sunlight, seemed to typify the day.

Trying to calm herself, Renee gave a whimper and a weak nod. "Thanks, Lacey. I'm sorry. Thanks." As she reached for Lacey for a second hug, Lacey patted her on the back. But Lacey was really a bit annoyed. Being the only one who knew about Renée and her past problems was getting to be a strain on Lacey. She had enough on her plate already.

"Shhh. Everything will be just fine," she reiterated. What she wanted to say was more like, Will you stop tugging at my dress? It's a one of a kind, and it cost a fortune. And you better not muss up my hair! But Lacey was trying her hardest today to show her best side. This was not the time or place to let her temper fly.

She pulled herself from Renée and motioned to Doug to take over. "I think she needs your help, Doug. Why don't you take her home?"

"Sure, Lacey. Whatever you say." It looked as if Doug, too, had reached sensory overload. He went through the motions, giving Lacey a hug and gathering up Renée. Lacey shook her head in disbelief as she watched the two make their exit. She wondered what had ever possessed her to allow Renée to become a Pink. She was so out to lunch. Sure, she was one of the tallest, prettiest, wildest girls at school, but she was an emotional basket case.

"Hey, Lacey, look!" Penny whispered, pulling a pink chiffon scarf out of her black handbag, making sure only Lacey would see it. "What do you think?"

"I think you shouldn't be so afraid to show our favorite color," Lacey was quick to answer. "It goes great with the outfit. But your makeup is a mess, darling. You really should tend to it."

"You're right, Lacey," Penny said with an embarrassed little smile. "What would I do without you?" She replaced the scarf and pulled out a compact and tissue. "I don't know what got into me back there," she remarked, futilely dabbing away at her pink nose and blotched cheeks. "I mean, April Lovewell and I weren't exactly best friends. We were more like this." She threw back her head and laughed sharply as she held up one hand, the first two fingers spread in a wide *V*.

Penny dropped her hand abruptly and her smile faded as she took in the astonished faces around her. Was another Pink about to go off the deep end? Lacey wondered. Penny could be a little tacky sometimes, but this was the sort of crack Lacey expected from Eddie Hagenspitzel, school dork.

"I guess I was hoping funeral season was over for me," Penny said, fighting to hold back tears.

Now Lacey felt truly bad for Penny. It seemed as

if the funeral for Penny's baby sister, who had tragically died from a crib death suffocation, was just yesterday. The shock of losing her only sibling was so great that Penny could barely speak for months. Lacey figured it was even more painful for Penny because she was adopted. Her parents had been elated to have finally succeeded in producing a "miracle baby," and Penny had a real baby sister to fuss over. It was like a dream for the whole Bolton family. To see it all shatter so suddenly must have been more than they could handle. Penny probably was reexperiencing the tragedy once again at April's funeral.

"You're amazing, Penny," Lacey said. "I'll bet you're feeling worse than most of us put together, and you've kept your sense of humor intact. Way to go, kid."

"Thanks, Lacey. I'm trying." Penny spoke softly. "Hey, Lacey, I know this sounds weird and all, but maybe things are just meant to be, you know? I mean, well, I know it's horrible what happened to April, but I guess now they'll have to choose a new Peach Blossom Queen. You'll be a shoo-in. You'll look great wearing that crown. Don't you think so, Hal?"

"Uh, sure," Hal said uneasily. "Life can be weird, I guess. Even in Paradiso."

Lacey winced inwardly. True, the same thought

about the Peach Blossom competition had flitted through her head about a hundred times, but to mention it here could hurt Lacey's chances.

She turned to hug Penny good-bye and hurry her departure along. As Hal and Penny turned to leave, Lacey reminded Penny, "Don't be bashful about wearing that scarf, huh? No reason not to add a bit of hope to the situation."

Penny looked back and smiled, pulling the scarf from her purse and draping it over her shoulder as Hal took her by the arm and walked her away. "Love ya, Lacey," she called as they made their way through the crowd.

Lacey looked around at the rest of the mourners. Look at 'em all, she thought. The whole town is here. Was April really this popular? Peach Blossom April?

Lacey was still in shock over that one. She thought again about the committee having to choose a new Queen and felt a strange pang in her stomach. Her feelings were all over the place. Poor, silly, loyal April was dead before she'd even finished high school. At the same time Lacey was still mad at April for stealing the crown from her. After all, April wouldn't even have been a candidate if Lacey hadn't campaigned for her. Having April in the contest was supposed to mean weaker competition, which could only have meant more votes for Lacey.

It was an ingenious plan. So conniving. How could it possibly have backfired?

And why do I feel so guilty? she thought. It's only natural. My whole life depended on winning. It was my stepping-stone to stardom. Madonna, move over, honey!

"You'll look great wearing that crown," she could hear Penny saying to her.

Penny just might be right. Crazy, but right, Lacey figured. Could April have died to help pave the road to my success? Stranger things have happened. And if April is resting peacefully, she's looking down at Paradiso cheering me on. I'm sure of it.

Still, the thought of riding to stardom on April's murder seemed a cruel twist. Even for Lacey.

She took a big deep breath and tried to exhale all the confusion away. No such luck. To make matters worse she noticed Manuel, her father's chauffeur, making his way through the crowd. No doubt he had been sent to fetch her. Daddy calls, Lacey comes, she thought. *Or else.* The welts on the backs of her legs seemed to swell up like balloons. She looked down to make sure that her dress still shielded the bruises from public view.

Manuel politely made his way toward Lacey, saying, "Excuse me, sir; *me permite*, señora," to practically everyone. "Señorita." He greeted her with a gentle, sympathetic smile. "I'm sorry, Señorita

22

Lacey, but your father insists that you leave now. He says he can't wait any longer and would like for you to return to the house together."

Lacey looked at her father, standing by the limo. He was simultaneously looking at his watch, looking for Lacey, and talking on his mobile phone. Always so busy. Everything so crucial.

Mother's demands were easily ignored. But Daddy's? That was another story. Without even an ounce of a struggle, she followed Manuel back to the limo like a lamb to the slaughter. Not today, Daddy, please not today.

When she got to the limo, Calvin Pinkerton, THE Calvin Pinkerton, chairman of Pinkerton Canneries and lord of Paradiso, was not as rushed as she had figured. Mother made up for it, however. She sat in the car, furious to have been so delayed by Lacey's tardiness.

"Lacey, please get in the car. Let's go," she hissed.

But Calvin Pinkerton put the phone down for a moment and held his daughter close. He turned to his wife and gave her such a look that it didn't take a word to quiet her down.

"There, there, sweetie," he said in a soothing tone. He hugged Lacey like his cherished princess. "I know how upset you must be. Come on, baby, we'll go home and rest a bit and maybe we'll feel a little better. Okay?"

"Sure, Daddy." Lacey felt a lot better.

"How would you like to have dinner at your favorite restaurant in San Francisco? Why not? We'll go home, Daddy will do a little work, and then we'll fly up, just the two of us. I'll have Manuel make arrangements to get the plane ready. What do you say, precious?"

"I love you, Daddy, really I do." As she wrapped her arms around him, Lacey hoped he was sincere this time. Could this be more than just another public display of affection? Maybe April's death had shaken him up a bit too. This could change everything. She knew he loved her more than anything. A stream of tears, a mixture of hope and fright, ran down her face. As her father handed her gently in the back of the limo, Lacey prayed that she could be part of a happy, loving family.

"Roll up these damn windows and let's get some AC going." Darla Pinkerton was her usual self, barking orders at Manuel.

"Of course, Señora Pinkerton." Obediently he hit the switch and the windows rolled to a tight close, creating an overbearing silence inside the car.

Lacey tensed and found herself wishing Mom hadn't skipped her usual Bloody Mary with breakfast. How weird, she thought, that a few drinks

24

always somehow mellowed Darla's bitchiness—at times to the point of making her seem almost spineless—while with Daddy . . .

She caught herself. No, she didn't want to think about the monster dear, sweet Daddy turned into when *he* drank.

Lacey pressed her nose against the glass to watch all the commotion as the limo slowly made its way out of the cemetery. The path out snaked its way around the grounds, giving Lacey a view from all directions.

She knew everyone. And she had something to say about them all. In the middle of the crowd she spotted Kiki De Santis. She felt a sharp stab as she thought about how they hadn't even spoken to each other since before April had been killed. Lacey remembered the fight they had had over the Peach Blossom Queen contest. Kiki was supposed to drop out of the running to swing more votes Lacey's way. Only Kiki had some farfetched idea that she might win, so she'd defied Lacey's request and the whole thing had gotten way out of hand. Kiki had been Lacey's best friend. How could they have become so estranged at a time like this?

As she watched the De Santises from the window, she realized what a close-knit family Kiki had. I wish I could get out of the car right now and spend the rest of the day with Kiki, she thought. It would be great for the Pinks to hang out by her pool and drink iced tea all afternoon. Lacey was still as mad as ever at Kiki, but she knew Kiki would come around and apologize and things would be back to normal.

As the limo rolled by, Lacey was sure that Kiki took notice. It seemed the two even made eye contact, each one wanting to wink or wave to the other but neither willing to break down. At least it was a start! Then Lacey realized no one could see into the limo. From the outside, the windows were completely black.

The limo rolled on. Past Raven Cruz and Vaughn Cutter—holding hands! The nerve of that chick to move in on my turf, Lacey steamed. Maybe she has style, but she and Vaughn are like night and day. What a couple! They can't be serious. I'll get him back in a second if I want.

And she noticed Jess Gardner standing with them. Probably the most handsome boyfriend Lacey had ever had. Was it a mistake to break up with him over Michelle Wheeler? Maybe I should have trusted him a little more, she thought. She still had trouble keeping her eyes off his beautifully sculpted swimmer's body, and she didn't want to keep her hands off it either. Maybe that cutie pie deserved a second chance.

As the limo reached the main road, Lacey took

one more look behind her. She saw two more boys from her class, whom she had etched in her memory as boyfriends number five and seven. Or was it four and six? She saw Doug Mattinsky's brother, Mitch, and remembered her first real kiss, the first night of summer vacation at Kiki's annual end-of-school pool party, freshman year.

"Well," said Lacey's mother, "now that *that* little spectacle is behind us, maybe someone will remember there's a Peach Blossom Festival coming, and we can get on with the election of a Queen."

She spoke as if April hadn't already been chosen, as if the election for Peach Blossom Queen hadn't already taken place.

Lacey thought again of what Penny had said about the contest. Then a darker thought came to her: If April had died to help Lacey become Peach Blossom Queen, was it possible that someone had helped April to help Lacey—by killing her for just that reason? Maybe someone who once had been a Peach Blossom Queen herself and couldn't stand for her legacy to be shattered, someone who would feel humiliated if the world knew she had produced a daughter unworthy of following in her footsteps. . . .

Lacey remembered when she was in the eighth grade and was trying out for the cheerleader squad, Mom being so determined that she get picked.

Darla had even gone so far as to befriend Coach Powers's mousey little wife, inviting Mrs. Powers to lunch, even flying her to San Francisco on the Pinkertons' private jet for a shopping spree at I. Magnin's. When Lacey, after all that, *didn't* get picked, Darla had been furious. Lacey would never be able to wipe the image from her mind of Mrs. Powers dropping by to see her new "best" friend, her eager smile crumpling, the color draining from her face as Darla screamed at her, "It's all your fault! If you cared about me at all you would have made sure Lacey got chosen. *I never want to see you again!*" Not long after that it was rumored that Mrs. Powers had some kind of nervous breakdown.

Could the same woman who so cruelly manipulated Mrs. Powers for her daughter's supposed sake have done away with April?

Lacey shook the absurd notion out of her head. Her thoughts were a confused blur. She was tired. It had been such a long day. It seemed as if this day had gone on forever.

CHAPTER 3

Hope stared at the small jail cell in the sheriff's office. Behind the bars, it was empty. It should have held an occupant. April's killer.

Hope sat across from Sheriff Rodriguez's desk and bit her nails nervously. She'd never given a statement to the police before. It wasn't as if Sheriff Rodriguez were a stranger. He had helped get Hope's cat, Gidget, out of trees on numerous occasions, and he'd addressed her class on drug and alcohol abuse every year since junior high. But this was different.

"I would have liked to talk to you right away," Sheriff Rodriguez said, putting a sturdy, rubber-soled shoe up on his desk, "but I know this has been a terrible shock to you. You must be very, very upset." Hope felt the intensity of his gaze as he scrutinized her. *Her!*

"Sheriff, you don't think, ah, that, I mean people

aren't saying that I might have been the one who . . ." Hope couldn't even put the sentence together. She was exhausted and numb. She'd barely slept the night before, and the idea that she could be the killer was too absurd.

But Sheriff Rodriguez had a serious look on his round, thick-featured face. "People are saying all kinds of things, Hope." His voice was matter-of-fact, but not without a note of kindness.

People. Hope had the unpleasant feeling that "people" meant Uncle Ward and Aunt Sara. "I think I know who you're talking about," she said. Her voice came out hurt and angry.

"Hope," the sheriff said gently, "they're in pain. They're scared. You expect to bury your parents, but not your children. They can't believe it. I can't believe it." He tipped himself back in his chair, the empty cell behind him. "Besides, if you look at it their way, the body was in your locker. And everybody knows your families had some bad blood between them."

Hope felt her temper rising. "Sheriff Rodriguez, April Lovewell was my best friend." Her words shook. It hurt just to say April's name out loud. "You can't seriously think I'm a suspect."

Sheriff Rodriguez's face creased into a frown. "There are no suspects. Yet. And no one's guilty until it's been proven. But I'm afraid in a little town like Paradiso, no one's innocent until proven innocent, either."

"Well, I do have proof," Hope said tightly. "I was working on my computer that night. You can check and see when I logged onto my electronic bulletin board. And when I logged off."

"I'm glad," the sheriff said quietly. "But I'm not surprised. It's just difficult to sort out the facts from the rumors." His gaze went to the newspaper on his desk.

Hope leaned forward to look at it. The Paradiso *Record.* Willa Flicker's twice-weekly paper that loved anything down and dirty. On the front page was a huge photo of April—the one she'd used in last year's yearbook. Hope stiffened as she looked at her cousin's big, generous smile. Her throat stung and she swallowed hard.

Under the picture of April were three smaller pictures: Lacey, Raven, and Kiki. Raven's and Kiki's pictures were also from their junior-year yearbook. The picture of Lacey was a newer photo; soft, pale bangs framed her face—it was a cut she'd gotten just recently. The background was all swirly and cotton-candy-like, and she looked drop-dead glamorous and done up. Probably some studio shot by a professional photographer her father had hired to take pictures of his princess.

The headline under the photos screamed WHO

DUNNIT? JEALOUS LOSER FOR PEACH BLOSSOM QUEEN? OR SOMEONE ELSE YOU KNOW?

Hope wanted to march into Willa Flicker's office and demand that she print an apology. The sheer nerve of her, to use April's death to pump a juicy story and inflate her own career. Hope was mad. Mad and miserable. She felt a warm tear run down her cheek without even realizing she'd shed it.

"Hey, hey," Sheriff Rodriguez murmured. "We're all upset. All on edge." He took his heavy shoe off the desk, got up, and came around to where Hope sat. He put a hand on her shoulder. "Hope, we don't have to do this right now if you don't want. You can give me your statement some other time." He paused. "But you're really the right person to help me out here, because you knew her best. You know, I've been on the force for twenty-some years now, but this is the first murder case I've ever had. If I can't get to the bottom of it, they're going to call in the big boys from Sacramento and take over my town. I could use your help. Smart girl like you. Principal Appleby tells me you're headed east to MIT in the fall."

Hope gulped back the tears and nodded, wiping her face with the sleeve of her sky blue sweatshirt. College was the last thing on her mind.

"So how about it?" the sheriff prompted. "Will you give me your statement now?"

Hope sniffled. "Yeah, sure," she said. "I want to find the person who did this as soon as possible. Get him locked up for good. Where do you want me to start?"

"Well, let me turn on my tape recorder here, and then I want you to tell me, in your own words, exactly what happened last Friday. And also whether your cousin was acting strange in any way before she was killed. Was there anything she was worried or unhappy about?"

Hope feared the answer would show on her face. The day of the murder, April had told Hope she needed to talk to her. In private. Some big secret. Hope couldn't imagine what it might have been. April had nothing to hide, as far as she knew. But if anything bad came out about April, Hope didn't think she could stand it. If there was even a hint of something, Willa Flicker would probably smear April's name all over the front of the *Record*. With April not even cold in her grave.

Should she tell Sheriff Rodriguez? He was the law. Still, maybe if she could find out what it was first. . . . Maybe Spike would know. Yeah, she would ask Spike. If she could find Spike.

She didn't know where to begin. Hope, known as a computer whiz, and Spike, a biker who spent most of his day in the vocational wing, didn't run much with the same crowd.

But then, Spike didn't really run with any particular crowd. When he wasn't helping out at home or working on his Harley, he usually was with April.

Most of the kids at school knew about the two of them, but they kept it pretty quiet. You just didn't squeal to adults about that kind of thing, no matter what you thought of the two people involved. It was an unwritten law. Hope doubted that Sheriff Rodriguez knew about April and Spike.

Under the awful, horrible circumstances, one part of her felt she ought to tell him. The other part was honor bound to keep quiet. Well. Maybe she would say something. But after she had had a chance to talk to Spike herself.

Hope watched Sheriff Rodriguez turn on his tape recorder and position it in front of her. She cleared her throat. "I—ah, on the morning of May 26, I—" In her mind, she saw April's lifeless arm dangling from her locker. She choked on her sentence.

The sheriff waited for her to regain her composure. "Hope," he said. "In your own words. Whatever's easiest for you. I'm not expecting you to compose a police memo."

Hope nodded. She squeezed her eyes shut, trying to squeeze out the picture of her locker, but it wouldn't go away. She had to go to school right after this, too, and see it. She took a deep, shaky breath and shrugged. "There's really nothing to tell that you don't already know. I went to school on Friday, opened up my locker, and—and my cousin's body fell out," she finished in a rush, not wanting to even hear the ugly words hanging in the air for longer than necessary.

Sheriff Rodriguez didn't turn off the tape recorder. "How about before that? You got up and got ready for school that morning. . . ." he prompted.

Hope sighed. "It was just like every other morning. I had breakfast. My mother made her usual comment about how I can pack it away. We said good-bye. She went to work, and I went to school."

"By car?"

Hope shook her head. "I walked. I like to walk. Anyway, the first thing that happened was I saw Dwight the—Principal Appleby on the school lawn and I talked him into telling me who had won Pretty Peggy Sue. I was so happy." Hope bit her lip. It had seemed like the beginning of a really special day. "Well, then I started going to my locker."

"Did you talk to anyone on the way?" Sheriff Rodriguez asked.

"Um—Eddie Hagenspitzel. And Jess. Jess Gardner. That's all, I think. I was kind of running. I was late."

"And then?"

"Then—that's it. Then I opened my locker. The next thing I knew, I was coming to in Jess's arms. I'd fainted."

"Jess Gardner," said the sheriff. "Is he your boyfriend?"

Hope was glad the tape recorder couldn't record her blush. "Just a friend," she said.

"I see. And is there anything else you want to tell me about April?" the sheriff asked.

April. April, who would never be able to speak for herself again. Hope felt the tears welling up in her eyes. "Sheriff Rodriguez, I don't know why anyone would want to murder my cousin." She felt her lips tremble. "Don't you have any clues at all?"

"Well . . . we've confirmed the cause of death. Also that April was hit on the head with a blunt instrument before she was strangled."

A cry rose in Hope's throat. The facts were so brutal. A wave of nausea came over her. She sank her face into her hands and prayed that April had been knocked out right away. At the very least, this: that it had been fast and painless.

"Maybe," said Sheriff Rodriguez, "I shouldn't be telling you this. It's too hard on you."

Hope pulled herself together. "No, sheriff. I want to know. Maybe there's something I can do to help find the person who killed my cousin." Hope glanced again at the cell behind the sheriff. It was a crime in itself that whoever had done this heinous thing was still out there. And might strike again.

Hope felt her pain and anger give way to fear. April was dead. And nobody knew who had killed her or why. Would there be another dead body before the killer was found? Hope shivered at the thought that the town she'd lived in all her life might be a stalking ground for the monster who had murdered April.

"We've got to find out what happened," she said to the sheriff. "Don't you know anything else?"

"I'm afraid not. But we'll have a full autopsy report in soon. Maybe that will turn up something new. Oh, there was one more thing. A footprint was found in the mud in front of the side door of the school."

"You mean the door that leads to the stairwell near the lockers? But that door is always locked. No one uses it."

"Someone did," the sheriff said. "The night of the murder. Deputy Sheriff Griffin and I found it open on Friday morning."

"Wow," Hope said seriously. "And you got a footprint?"

"Well, a piece of one. Might have had a whole set if it hadn't rained Thursday night. But the print closest to the door was sheltered by the building, at least partially. Looks like a man's sneaker."

"A man's? You can tell that from the print?"

"The size. Too big for a woman. We made a plaster cast and it's being analyzed. Maybe we can find out exactly what kind of shoe made it. That's all—we have nothing more to go on."

"Yet," Hope added, with grim determination. She was going to go right home after school and enter every shred of information in her computer. She wasn't sure how it would help, but her computer had always helped her sort things out before.

Still, how could a machine sort out her bitter emotions? April was gone. Uncle Ward was making hysterical accusations about Hope. And Paradiso, California, had become a dangerous place to live.

Sheriff Rodriguez turned off the tape recorder. "I think that's all. Thank you, Hope."

"Sure," Hope said, getting up. "Will you tell me as soon as you find out anything else? Even the littlest thing?"

Sheriff Rodriguez nodded. "Oh, and Hope? Those records that show you were working on your computer Thursday night? I'll be needing a copy of them. Just as a formality, of course."

"Of course." But Hope knew what that meant. Anyone in Paradiso might be a suspect. Or the next victim.

CHAPTER 4

The locker gleamed. It was shiny clean, and the smell of ammonia burned all the way down the hall. A group of kids had gathered around it and were staring, as if the latest music video were previewing on the locker door.

Raven shuddered. Normally, she wasn't the least bit squeamish. Not after all the diapers she'd changed on her little brothers and sisters. Not after plucking chickens and cleaving pork chops at the café for years. Raven had no patience with oh-no-it's-a-bug-eek! girls. But the squeaky cleanness of Hope Hubbard's locker, the brand-new, scrubbed-extra-well cleanness, only pointed out the sordidness of the deed that had been done. It was impossible not to feel queasy when you looked at the shiny locker.

Or, as Lady Macbeth said, "Out, damn'd spot!"

They were reading *Macbeth* in Raven's English class. A creepily appropriate choice. What would Shakespeare have made of the murder in Paradiso?

Raven joined the crowd, edging in next to Kiki De Santis. "Poor April," Kiki said to her.

"Well," boomed out Eddie Hagenspitzel, his voice as big as the rest of him, "at least she was queen for a day!"

A few nervous twitters went through the crowd, but Eddie didn't get as many laughs as usual.

"It's no joke, Eddie," said Renée Henderson. "This is serious. Dead serious." Raven noticed how pale Renée looked, and how tired. There were deep, dark circles under her eyes, and her voice was shaky.

"Yeah," Kiki seconded. "April's gone, and there's a killer on the loose." She toyed nervously with her long brown hair, her hazel eyes wide and scared.

"One of us might be the next one to fall out of a locker," someone else said.

"Can you imagine having to be the one to clean that thing out?" Janice Campbell whined.

"Eew," Emily Gilman commented.

"Can you imagine what kind of sicko stuffed her in there in the first place?" Doug Mattinsky asked. Next to him, Renée shook noticeably.

Raven wondered the same thing. Who on earth

would do something like this? What kind of sub-person? In *Macbeth*, Macbeth and Lady Macbeth killed King Duncan so that they could take over the throne. Some people were saying similar things about April's killer. That it was one of the girls who had lost the contest for Peach Blossom Queen.

Well, there were exactly three losers: Raven, Kiki, and Lacey. Raven mentally crossed her own name off the list. Then she crossed off Kiki. She didn't have any proof, but she didn't need it. She'd gotten to know Kiki a lot better during the contest, and she knew Kiki didn't have a vicious bone in her body.

Not too long ago, Raven had thought that Kiki was just another Lacey Pinkerton wannabe, smug about being one of Lacey's cherished Pinks and tagging along with Lacey to Sacramento or San Francisco to be seen at the latest clubs. It was true that Kiki liked to have a good time, but Raven had discovered Kiki was really down to earth, too. And genuinely nice. If Kiki had one fault, it was that she let Lacey influence her too much. At least, she had until their big fight the week before. Since then, they'd barely spoken.

Lacey—now there was someone who would stop at nothing to be Queen. Raven thought about all the times Lacey had come into Rosa's for an iced tea with lemon before school—and to get in a few digs as Raven fed the chickens or rushed around in her waitress uniform, trying to stay on top of the breakfast crowd.

"Gee, you really work hard to pull yourself out of the trenches," Lacey had once said in her most saccharine tones. It was right after Raven had gotten her picture in the *Record* in an article on fashion in Paradiso. In the photograph she wore a one-sleeve tank dress she'd copied from *Vogue*. Yeah, it was a great dress, but Raven could think of more important things you could do to get your picture in the paper. And better papers than the *Record*, too. Still, it was clear that Lacey wished she'd been the one to grace the paper's pages.

"I think she'd like to kill you," Raven's friend Denise Guthrie had said more than once.

But Raven didn't honestly think Lacey would kill anyone. She was just selfish, not a murderer. So who had done it? Nobody at Paradiso High *seemed* like a murderer. Not even school psycho Bubba Dole. Raven stared at the newly clean locker.

"Ugh. It makes you want to go home and bolt all the doors and never come out," said Bobby Deeter, joining the crowd and slinging a protective arm around Kiki.

Kiki let Bobby pull her close, but she didn't respond by putting her own arm around him. Raven got the feeling that Kiki wasn't as crazy about

Bobby as he was about her. She wondered if Kiki was staying with him just to avoid hurting his feelings.

Funny, Raven thought, how feelings can change seemingly overnight. Look at Kiki and Lacey. And wasn't it just a few weeks ago that she'd heard Kiki say she couldn't imagine *ever* breaking up with Bobby? Could this new cooling-off Raven sensed on Kiki's part have anything to do with Kiki's newfound independence? Something in Kiki had changed since her break with Lacey and the Pinks. Raven had admired the way she'd stood her ground, done what she thought was right despite the consequences. Maybe Kiki was ready to take more chances—including looking for a new boyfriend. Bobby was sweet, dependable, considerate, and, Raven thought, probably a little bit boring. Raven pictured Kiki with someone more mysterious and challenging.

"You're right, Bobby," Emily Gilman said breathily. "I got the creeps just walking to school today. Speaking of which," she added, turning to Raven, "I know I said I'd help collect more signatures for your Stop the Greenway Mall petition, but I don't think I really want to go around door to door anymore."

"Yeah, maybe it's not a great idea," Flora Mendoza chimed in.

Raven stifled a groan. She could see her most important project dying before her eyes. Raven's dream was to be an environmental lawyer, and this was her first big battle. "Hey, guys, don't bag out on me now!" Her hand automatically went to the green SCAM button on her T-shirt—Students Concerned About the Mall. The black letters were shaded by a leafy tree. "Do you really want to see the scrublands turned into a parking lot?"

"No, but I don't want to see another dead body, either," Emily said.

"You didn't see it, Emily," Raven pointed out. It came out more brusquely than she'd meant it. But she couldn't let SCAM get buried too.

"You know what I mean," Emily answered.

Raven softened. "Yeah. I do. But we can't allow Calvin Pinkerton and his Greenway Mall to win. That would be another kind of crime. I mean, it's people like him who are destroying the environment, putting holes in the ozone layer, speeding up the greenhouse effect. Why? For some pieces of green paper."

"All right!" said a new voice. Vaughn. Raven smiled for the first time all day. Vaughn's dad was Calvin Pinkerton's partner on the mall project, but Vaughn had "gone over to the other side," as he liked to put it. "Better-looking team captain, among other things," he'd joked to Raven.

Raven eased into Vaughn's strong hug. The guy was so hot!

She remembered when the mere thought of having a steady boyfriend had once seemed as remote as her winning the Peach Blossom Queen title. For one thing, she hadn't really *wanted* to get this close to any guy. Between knocking herself out to get the 4.0 average she'd need to qualify for a scholarship to a good college, and helping Mama and Papa at the diner, who even had time? Besides, most of the guys she'd dated were so annoyingly macho, expecting her to agree with everything they said, and wanting to tie her up with a little pink bow. What she loved best about Vaughn was that he wasn't intimidated by her being so independent, and when she really was too busy to see him, he didn't sulk about it. He understood that not in a million years could she ever be an eye-batting, game-playing princess like Lacey Pinkerton. She, Raven, had an opinion on nearly every subject, and seldom failed to speak her mind. And Vaughn, though she knew she went overboard at times, just *accepted* her, prickles and all.

"Some of your sailors jumping ship?" Vaughn asked.

Raven looked into his blue eyes and nodded. "A case of the serious creeps."

"Can't blame anyone," Vaughn said. "Still, we

don't have time to wait for this to blow over. We'll just have to collect signatures in groups to be safer. Kiki and I were supposed to do Winding Hill Road together anyway. Right, Keeks?" Vaughn and Kiki were neighbors up on the fashionable Hill, as it was called.

Kiki looked a trifle nervous, but she nodded. "You can count on me, Raven."

"And me," said Winston Purdy III, raising his hand and in the process knocking his glasses off his nose. Good old Winston. Okay, he was a major nerd, but his heart was in the right place. "We've gotta stick together," he said.

"Now more than ever," Raven agreed. "How about you, Emily? Will you change your mind?"

Emily studied the floor. "I don't know . . ." she said. "There's a killer in Paradiso. A psychopath. A murderer. It could be anyone."

Nobody said a word. The tension around Hope's locker was so thick you could almost touch it. People were looking around at each other suspiciously.

Renée Henderson let out a low moan. "I can't take it! I just can't!" She broke away from the crowd of kids and went running down the hall. Doug Mattinsky ran after her.

"Whoa, is her house on fire?" Penny Bolton asked. "Or does she know something about this that she's not telling?"

Raven felt her temperature rise. No wonder Penny's nickname was "the Mouth." Raven measured her response to Penny. The last thing anyone needed right now was nasty rumors. But before she said anything, she was distracted by a loud, snarling voice.

"Outta my way!" yelled Bubba Dole, heading straight for the crowd in front of the lockers. Bubba was small and wiry, but he was one mean guy. Raven jumped aside, getting out of Bubba's line of fire.

"Yo, dude, what's with you?" Eddie Hagenspitzel yelled.

Bubba kept moving, a nasty little bulldozer.

"I think his locker's next to Hope's," Kiki said, quickly stepping to the side, next to Raven.

It all happened in a blur. Somehow, Winston didn't get out of the way fast enough. Before Raven knew what was going on, Bubba had Winston pinned up against Hope's locker—that shiny clean, gruesome reminder of a locker. Bubba yanked Winston's glasses and flung them down the hall. Someone screamed. Winston hung from Bubba's clenched fists, his feet dangling inches off the floor. He looked terrified, as if he'd just seen April's body.

Vaughn stepped toward them. His square jaw was set as hard as steel, and his eyes were like ice.

"Bubba, let him go," he warned through gritted teeth.

Bubba didn't blink. He simply opened up his hands and dropped Winston to the ground. "Okay," he said. Without glancing down at Winston or over at Vaughn, Bubba started dialing the combination on the locker next to Hope's.

Raven recalled the rumors she had heard around school last year. Vaughn supposedly had been so furious with Bubba once that he cracked Bubba's skull open. From the looks of things, the rumors were true. But Vaughn's fury faded as quickly as it had appeared. He leaned down to help Winston. "You all right?"

Winston nodded shakily as he got up.

People moved off down the hall, away from Bubba.

"Boy, Psycho knows how to break up a party," Raven said softly, out of Bubba's hearing. "Come on, Winston, we'll walk you to your first class."

"I guess Bubba doesn't go in much for sticking together," Winston tried to joke as they went down the corridor.

Raven frowned. It was going to be next to impossible to keep people together with all the fear and suspicion that had descended over Paradiso.

"Are you okay?" Vaughn asked after they had dropped Winston off at his AP calculus class.

Raven shrugged. "I didn't know you had a temper like that. I never saw it before."

Vaughn reached down and cupped Raven's chin in his hand. "I'm sorry, babe. It's just that when something gets me mad, it gets me really mad. I'm usually pretty calm, but there's not any in between with me. Hey, I didn't scare you, did I? You know I could never feel like that with you."

Raven smiled. "I know. There's other stuff on my mind, too. What I'm scared of is that while people's minds are somewhere else, a cement truck's going to roll right over the scrublands, and no one's going to notice." She played with her jangly bracelets. "Plus, I feel like a really terrible person for worrying about the mall when April's just been killed. I mean, I'm going to miss her. I really am . . ." Raven could feel the tears gathering behind her eyes.

"Shhh," Vaughn murmured as he pulled Raven close, right in the middle of the hall. "Shh. It's all right. Of course you're going to miss her. But life can't stop because of this. I mean, we've all got to live a little extra for April, right? You've gotta work even harder to stop the mall. April would have wanted it."

Raven wrapped her arms around Vaughn's shoulders. She could feel his well-defined wrestler's muscles through his oxford-cloth shirt. "Yeah, you're right," she said. "April loved the scrublands. She was doing a series of sketches there, before—" Her voice wavered and the tears that had been gathering streamed down her cheeks.

Vaughn took her face in his hands. "I'm gonna miss her too," he said huskily. "But we'll help each other through."

Raven felt the warmth of his hands. She breathed in his nearness. Her mouth met his, and their tears mingled with the moist warmth of their kiss. For that moment, Raven's worries slipped away.

CHAPTER 5

The first thing Lacey saw as she walked into Mr. Appleby's office was Kiki and Raven sitting side by side on a small couch. She knew immediately why she had been called down to the principal's office. For once it wasn't for bad-mouthing a teacher or skipping a class. Lacey was sure this meeting had been scheduled for them to talk about the Peach Blossom contest.

Lacey noticed that Mr. Appleby wasn't there. Just Kiki and Raven, looking awfully chummy with each other, their faces appropriately long for poor, dead April.

"And then there were three," Lacey intoned, in a fake ominous voice. "Or better put," she chided, "the two musketeers and the Peach Blossom Queen."

Lacey was in rare form. Maybe it had just taken

a good night's sleep. She felt well rested and together, ready to take on by storm Paradiso, the murder, the Peach Blossom Queen dilemma, or anything else that came her way. She had decked herself out in a brand-new pink top and matching designer tights that didn't hide any curves (but did, thank goodness, conceal the fading purple-and-yellow streaks on her legs). She could just see the alarm bell going off in both Raven and Kiki's heads. They eyed her warily as if to say that they knew she was up to her old tricks. Lacey felt a little buzz of satisfaction.

She took a seat in the soft leather chair behind Mr. Appleby's desk. "What's new, gals? Lovely pair of earrings, Kiki. Did your mom buy them for you, or are those studs an early graduation present from your grandmother? And real pearls, I'll bet." She paused and gave Raven the once-over. "And Raven, I see you've sewn up another winner. I think the shopping bag my outfit came in was made from the same material."

Lacey chuckled at her own remarks. She would have gone on, but she was interrupted by Dwight Appleby, who entered his office carrying a large stack of papers and books. The principal was barely visible behind all the things piled in his arms. He stumbled and proceeded to drop his entire bundle of stuff right on Lacey's lap.

"Oh, my . . . oops, um . . . Oh, I'm so sorry . . . oops, my glasses. Oh, let me . . ." Embarrassingly he fumbled over Lacey and collected his things.

"Please, Mr. Appleby, don't worry. Let me get that." Lacey seized the opportunity to sweet talk. After all, Mr. Appleby was an important member of the Peach Blossom Queen selection committee. In her best innocent-little-girl act Lacey helped him scoop up the papers and put them on his desk. She had all the moves down. She even picked up his horn-rimmed glasses, blew some dust off them, and reached up to put them back on top of his bald head. "There you are, sir," she said.

Then she plunked back down in his chair and watched with a playful eye as Mr. Appleby looked nervously for a place to sit. He finally leaned uncomfortably against a bookshelf in the corner of his office, coming close to knocking the whole thing over as he tried to balance himself.

"Oh, my! Please, Mr. Appleby. I didn't realize . . ." Lacey started to get up, but Mr. Appleby waved his hands in her direction.

"No, no. No, you stay there. It's cool," he insisted.

What a dweeb, Lacey thought.

Mr. Appleby tried to gain his composure. "I'm sorry I'm late. It's just that, well, with everything that's happened, it seems my job has gotten a bit crazy. I hope you haven't been waiting too long."

"Actually, Mr. Appleby, sir," Lacey began, "actually, I was late too. See, I was on my way to school and I was, of course, thinking about my friend April. Well, I decided to buy some fresh flowers for her, and I went to the cemetery to put them by her side. I just thought it was the right thing do." She removed the pink silk handkerchief from her bag as if preparing for a cry. "I thought I would make it to school on time, really I did, but I guess I must have stayed to visit April longer than I realized. I'm truly sorry."

She tried unsuccessfully to force a tear from her eyes. But she was sure her act had been bought by all, hook, line, and sinker. Kiki reached for her handkerchief, and Raven sniffled. Dwight the Dweeb was a believer too. Lacey watched him bury his head in his hands for a moment, as if all were lost. While he was out of it, Lacey swiveled in the leather chair, turning her back to Mr. Appleby, and stuck her tongue out at Kiki and Raven, giving them a sudden shock.

"Please, Lacey," Mr. Appleby said sympathetically. "I understand completely. Say no more. I'll tell you what," he proposed. "I'll sign a late pass for you if you'll do the same for me. Deal?"

They smiled at each other.

"Deal," she answered.

Lacey felt sure she was winning big points toward Pretty Peggy Sue. She knew Kiki or Raven wouldn't expose her for all her trickery. They'd just look bad themselves for trying. She had them all right where she wanted them.

Mr. Appleby began what must have been a rehearsed speech. "Well," he said, "I'm only sorry that my good fortune to have three of the prettiest, most vivacious girls, uh . . . women . . . uh . . . dudes . . . uh . . ."

"Anyway," he continued, "I'm sorry to have to meet with you under such tragic circumstances. But we need to talk about the Peach Blossom contest."

"Who's the winner?" Lacey blurted. She immediately bit her tongue. *Lacey, stay cool.*

"Well, actually," Mr. Appleby informed them, "there is no winner, yet. In fact, we may not have a contest at all."

Lacey's heart sank.

Mr. Appleby continued, "The committee has weighed the pros and cons and, well, that's why you're all here. I want to know what you guys think. I'd like you to help me make a decision. So, what do you say?"

"Yes! No! No! Yes! Yes! . . ." Everybody spoke at once.

"Hey, one at a time!" Mr. Appleby shouted.

They all blabbed again, "No! Yes! No! Yes! Yes!"

"Please!" he shouted again. "I promise, you'll all get a chance. Everyone's opinion interests me. Kiki, why don't you go first. What do you think, Ms. De Santis?"

Kiki looked down at the dishwater gray rug and began in a soft, faraway voice. "Well, I've thought about it a lot. And . . ." She paused and took a deep breath to gather confidence. "I think we already have a winner. April. April won the contest and is therefore the rightful Queen."

Lacey gave Kiki a cold, hard stare, but she couldn't get Kiki to look up at her.

Kiki took another deep breath and continued. "April Lovewell is the Peach Blossom Queen. Dead or alive!"

Kiki gathered strength and went on. "I was also thinking about the crown and the scholarship. I figure it must be worth a lot of money. Maybe we could use the money for a scholarship fund or a foundation in April's name. You know what I mean."

Mr. Appleby put a ponderous hand to his forehead. "Hmmm, a foundation? Hmmm. The April Lovewell Foundation. Better yet, the April Lovewell Peach Blossom Memorial Foundation. Has quite a ring to it, don't you think? Kiki, I can see why you were nominated for Peach Blossom Queen. You truly have a good heart."

Oh, brother, Lacey steamed. She's full of it! I'm sure she's earned some major points. Trying to sew up the Dweeb's vote, that's for sure.

At first, Lacey figured she'd have to resort to the same logic. But then she thought again and realized that if she did argue against the contest out of respect for April, the contest would definitely be canceled.

Instead, she opted for the "Lacey's-the-most-polite-little-girl-in-the-world" approach. "Well, sir, at first I felt the way Kiki did. But maybe we should consider the other side too. I think that the festival, with a crown, a ball, and a bar-no-expenses parade, may be just the thing this town needs to lift it out of this funk. We could all use that, don't you think? A little happiness just might make the sun shine in Paradiso again."

Lacey had captured Mr. Appleby's attention like an Oscar nominee. She had him focused intensely on her, waiting eagerly for her to continue. She stood up for extra effect, pretending she was on the debating team like Kiki's total yawn of a boyfriend, Bobby Deeter.

"Secondly," she stated, holding two fingers in the air, "consider April. What would April want? What would she think? If she couldn't use the crown, the scholarship, or the screen test, wouldn't she want me—I mean, one of *us* to have it?" Oops.

Damn! Lacey thought. Watch yourself, Lacey, you got 'em eating out of the palm of your hand. Don't blow it, girl!

She regained her composure and finished her argument. "I think April would say 'Yes! Go on with the show.' She'll be there in spirit partying with us all."

Academy award. Best performance.

"A-plus, Lacey." Mr. Appleby seemed convinced and nodded with approval. "I can also see why you were chosen as a candidate for Peach Blossom Queen. Yes, April. Never thought of what she would want. And hope restored to Paradiso. I didn't think it was possible. But maybe . . ."

Her voice filled with confidence, Raven spoke up. "Lacey's right. She's absolutely right. This may be the first time in my life that I, Raven Maria Cruz, will be on the same side as Lacey Pinkerton. I think that April would want it this way too. She would want one of us to go to college with that money." Raven looked straight at Mr. Appleby. "And to be frank, Mr. Appleby, that's what's most important to me, too. April's memory isn't going to be served by denying one of us of that chance."

"Hmmm, yes," muttered Mr. Appleby. "A

nominee concerned with education before stardom. I can see why you were voted in, Raven."

I can't believe her, Lacey thought. She's practically begging for the crown.

Raven continued, "And like Lacey said, maybe it would help us get over this tragedy."

"And maybe it would get us killed!" Kiki blurted. "Haven't you all noticed how scary this town has become? People are afraid to walk the streets alone. And when they do, they're looking over their shoulders every two seconds to make sure they aren't being stalked. There's a murderer in town." She buried her head in her hands and cried.

"I'm sorry," she said through the tears, "but I'm not sure I could go on with the contest. If I won, I might break down right in the middle of the parade."

Don't worry, kiddo, you don't stand a chance, Lacey thought.

Kiki calmed down a little. "And what if April didn't approve? I don't want her turning over in her grave."

"April would be psyched!" Lacey insisted. "And if you really feel that way, Kiki, then maybe you should drop out. You told me right at the start, even before April died, that you wanted to withdraw. Remember?"

Lacey saw how stunned Kiki was by her comment. Kiki's big hazel eyes flashed.

"I what!" Kiki said. "I never—"

But Mr. Appleby interrupted. "Now, now, Kiki. It's all right." He gave Kiki a soothing smile. "If we do feel it best to continue the contest, I would certainly understand your dropping out. I think everyone would. Don't feel it's a cop-out. Under the circumstances I would probably do the same."

"Mr. Appleby," Lacey put in, "excuse me, sir, but I don't think you would win the nomination. I mean, you're a great guy and all, but Peach Blossom Queen?"

Her joke broke the tension, and all of them cracked up. Even Kiki. Lacey saw that old laugh of hers, that mouth wide open displaying all those pearly whites. Lacey and Kiki's eyes met for the first time since their big fight. It was great to see Kiki laughing at one of her jokes again. But Kiki quickly turned her head away.

"Well," Mr. Appleby announced, "I know how you all feel, and I thank you for sharing your thoughts with me. You are all intelligent, beautiful, unique, and extremely thoughtful young ladies."

As he paused for a second, Lacey was on the edge of her seat.

He continued, "I think the committee will have a very tough time choosing Pretty Peggy Sue."

"Does that mean it's on?" Lacey asked, not quite believing she had heard correctly.

"We're on," he confirmed.

Phew, there's still hope for stardom, Lacey cheered silently. Kiki looked very unhappy.

"You know," Mr. Appleby said, "I've got radio station KPOP calling me every two minutes to find out what the verdict is. I think they've invested so much time and money in pumping up the contest they just might go broke if we canceled."

He looked directly at Kiki and continued. "Maybe we could get them to make a donation to the April Lovewell Foundation. And you know what, Kiki? The foundation is looking for a director. Interested?"

"You bet!" she answered.

Lacey was elated that the contest was on again. Now all she had to do was figure out how she was going to win Pretty Peggy Sue.

CHAPTER 6

Kiki spotted Lacey and the Pinks conspicuously seated at a table in the middle of the cafeteria. A rare gray, rainy day was keeping everybody inside, instead of out catching a few lunchtime rays on the front lawn as usual. A wide swath of empty seats was cut around the Pinks, as if people were afraid to come too close to Paradiso High's only remaining royal figure and her ladies-in-waiting. Last week, Kiki would have been one of those ladies, but now she determinedly walked away from them, searching the room for a friendly face. She could have eaten with Raven if Raven hadn't been off illicitly borrowing the Paradiso High *Grapevine*'s copier to run off more anti-Greenway petitions.

Kiki finally caught sight of Vaughn, also missing Raven, sitting with Jess Gardner and Bobby. She headed their way.

"Hi, Keeks," Vaughn said. "Welcome to the outer circle. Have a seat."

"Thanks." She returned Vaughn's sympathetic grin and sat down next to Bobby. Last week, they all would have been sitting with Lacey.

"Hiii, guys." A sharp, nasal voice shredded the air around them.

"Ugh. Surprise attack from the rear," Vaughn muttered.

"Hi, Penny," Kiki said softly. Penny looked at her, stared right through her for a long moment, then turned wordlessly to Vaughn.

"Mind if I sit down for a sec?"

"Free admission," Vaughn told her.

"So, Vaughn, have you heard the latest one that's flying through the halls of PHS?" Had Penny always been so mean and annoying? Had Kiki just failed to notice it in her blind loyalty to the Pinks? Or was Penny worse than ever because she had the story of a lifetime to spread her nasty gossip about?

"If it's a rumor about April," Vaughn said, "I'm not really interested."

"What if it's one about your best friend, Jess, and April?"

"Penny, I think your boss is calling," Vaughn said, motioning over his shoulder to Lacey's table.

"Wait," Jess said. "What are you talking about, Penny?" His hamburger froze in his hand, halfway

63

between his plate and his mouth, and a deep line creased his forehead.

Penny grinned like a dog who had just treed a cat twice its size. "I thought you might be interested," she singsonged. She leaned toward the center of the table and said in a stage whisper, "Some people are saying that the last time April Lovewell was seen alive, it was in your car. Driving out of town with *you*, Jess. The night she was *murdered.*"

Vaughn laughed harshly. "Bolton, you're sinking to a new low," he said. "Even for you. Isn't any subject safe from your trashy gossip?"

But Kiki noticed Jess wasn't laughing. He looked at Penny for a minute, then slowly bit into his hamburger, took a long chug from his milk carton, and shrugged. "Whoever's saying that is lying."

Penny shrugged back. "The person I heard sounded pretty sure. You were driving down Old Town Road. April was in the passenger seat. She was crying and trying to get out. But you were driving too fast. If she had jumped out, she might have killed herself. Course, if she had known what was coming . . ."

"Who saw that?" Jess said, his voice tight.

"I thought you said it didn't happen."

"It didn't. But I want to know who's spreading the lie." His voice was louder now, and he leaned toward Penny with anger in his eyes.

"Easy," Bobby said, putting a hand on Jess's arm to hold him back.

"Bolton," Vaughn said, his voice a low, menacing growl. "Get out of here. Now. And don't come back to spread any more of your dirt if you know what's good for you." Vaughn's face was a thundercloud about to roar open on a sizzling summer day.

Penny backed away from the table, her round eyes wide with astonishment and fear. But she couldn't resist having the last word. "I didn't make it up, so don't be mad at me. I'm just telling you, as a friend, what people are saying." For the first time since she arrived, she looked back at Kiki. "Of course, some people around here don't know the meaning of that word." She spun on her tiny sneaker-shod foot and bounced away.

Vaughn pushed back angrily from the table, the metal feet of his chair scraping noisily against the linoleum floor. "I'm taking off. I gotta get Raven and get out of here. I'll see you guys later."

"Me, too," said Jess, a little more calmly. "Sorry, guys. I'll see you."

As Jess left, Bobby looked gently at Kiki and put an arm around her, squeezing her shoulder protectively. "Bobby," Kiki said, looking into his eyes and already seeing pain there, as he guessed what she was about to say. "Bobby, I think I need to be alone for a while." His hand went slack on her shoulder, then dropped away. "I'm sorry. I'm just so confused. I'm gonna head out of here."

As Kiki got up, Bobby held her fingers for just a moment, then let them fall. "Bye, Keeks," he whispered.

"Bye, Bobby. I—I'll see you later."

Bobby raised one shoulder in a half shrug. "Whatever," he said, turning back to face his tray of fish sticks and french fries.

Kiki walked out of the cafeteria and down the corridor. She wasn't sure where she was going, but she had to get away from all the noise. The rumors were flying fast and thick about who had killed April and why, and who knew what. The one about Jess showed just how low people would go. Add in all the dramatically long expressions and moist eyes of the people who seemed to think this was some kind of contest to see who was closest to April and who was suffering the most. April probably would have taken a look around and sneaked off somewhere to do some sketching.

Kiki felt sorry for everyone who hurt, but she had had enough of a group meeting in Mr. Appleby's office; she hadn't been prepared for another one in the cafeteria. She'd make it up to Bobby by being extra nice when she saw him after school.

An image of April appeared in Kiki's mind—

April very much alive and well, holding a paint-brush in her hand during Mr. Woolery's art class.

"Wow! That's really great," Kiki had said, study-ing the canvas April had been painting of Spike. "It makes him look so—I don't know—"

"Dark and mysterious?" April had asked.

"Yeah. Right. Something about all those purple shadows."

April had laughed. "He was trying to memorize names and dates for a history test. Pretty mysteri-ous, huh?"

Kiki had laughed along. "Well, it's still a really cool painting. Mine is so—blah." She'd been trying to capture the view from her bedroom window at sunset, when the green hills of Paradiso rolled down into the darkening valley and the blue sky got streaky with magenta and orange. But Kiki couldn't get the perspective right, and the houses in the valley looked as if they had been transplanted from Winding Hill Road.

"Kiki, I like what you're painting," April had said. "I mean for starters, your colors are great. To go with your sneakers." Kiki had been wearing her lavender hightops that day. She had them on today too, in memory of the last time she'd seen April. "You just have to stop worrying about getting it *right* and try to get it the way you feel it." April

67

guided Kiki's arm to the canvas. "Loosen up, let the brush move more freely. Know what I'm saying?"

Kiki could almost hear April's voice echoing from the pale blue cinderblock walls around her. It made her feel better—as if April were with her, somehow. She wrinkled her brow. She was only sorry about the comment she'd made at the end of that class. *April, yours is so good, I'm going to strangle you.* Strangle! How could Kiki have uttered that terrible word? It had come out sounding so horribly jealous, when she'd meant it as a compliment. But April knew that, didn't she? Sure she did. She'd grinned at Kiki and said, "Oh, come on."

April. It just wasn't fair.

Kiki thought about the scene in Mr. Appleby's office. Maybe Raven and Lacey were right. April would have wanted the celebration to go on. But it was important to pay tribute to her memory, too. Kiki stared at her sneakers. "Your colors are great," she heard April's voice say again.

Suddenly Kiki knew exactly what she wanted to do. She turned and headed straight to the art room.

She pushed open the door and stopped in her tracks. Mr. Woolery, Paradiso's hunky art teacher, was sitting cross-legged on the floor in the middle of the room. April's paintings and drawings surrounded him, spread out like a picnic.

He looked up, startled. "Oh, uh, Kiki. Hi . . ."

He looked glassy eyed and exhausted, and he had several raw nicks on his handsome face where he'd cut himself shaving.

Wow. Mr. Woolery seemed as flipped out as some of his students. More, maybe.

"I didn't mean to disturb you," Kiki said, starting to back out of the room.

"No. It's okay. I was just—just looking over some of April's work." Some of it? It looked like a major retrospective to Kiki. Mr. Woolery had pushed the tables and chairs, the easels, and all the other furniture to the walls of the room so he could have enough space for April's art. In his hand, he held a pencil drawing. His hand shook, and the drawing fluttered.

"Mr. Woolery, are you okay?" Kiki asked.

He nodded. "Just upset. Sad. Like everyone else, I suppose."

"Yeah, I feel the same," Kiki said. She walked over to Mr. Woolery and looked at the sketch he was holding. "Oh, is that Spike?"

Mr. Woolery managed a little laugh. "That's what I thought, too. But April said she was trying to draw me."

Kiki studied the drawing. Mr. Woolery and Spike both had thick, dark hair, deep-set, dark eyes, and full mouths. But their noses were different, and they didn't really look that much alike. In real life it would be hard to confuse Mr. Woolery's Yankee-bred good looks with Spike's sexy, Latin handsomeness. Then Kiki remembered what April had said to her about painting the way you feel. Maybe with the way April had felt about Spike, all the guys she'd drawn had come out looking a little like him.

Spike. Where was he, anyway? Not in school—Kiki hadn't seen him around since last week. She could certainly understand his lying low. Spike was a quiet guy to begin with. And he must be feeling a heck of a lot worse than Kiki and Mr. Woolery put together.

Kiki walked around the edges of the room, looking at April's work. Now that was definitely Spike—there was the front tire of his Harley sneaking onto the edge of the page. And there were some watercolor sketches of the scrublands. The grasses bloomed in wild, loose brush strokes and delicate shades of greens and blues and violets. The scrubland paintings never would be finished. Kiki felt an overpowering wave of sadness.

Next to a charcoal sketch of a little red bird perched on a tree branch was a small portrait of April's parents, Reverend and Mrs. Lovewell. Their expressions were pinched, the tight lines in their faces darkened almost to a caricature. Bright yellow light caught the tops of their heads, like halos. Next to it was another picture of them—solemn, but somehow softer than the first drawing, and you could see that April really had loved them.

Then there was a quick sketch that Kiki remembered well. April had done it up in Kiki's bedroom when Kiki had invited her to spend the afternoon with the Pinks. April had seemed so happy to be part of the Pinks—even for the afternoon—that she had insisted on capturing it on paper.

Never mind that Lacey was just using April, egging her on because it fed her ego to have April tagging after her, aping her every move, even the way she wore her clothes. In the picture, Kiki, Lacey, Renée, and Penny were all squeezed onto Kiki's bed, eating chocolate chip cookies. Kiki and Lacey were grinning at each other with their mouths full. Better times.

As Kiki looked at the sketch, she felt the same confusion and loneliness that she'd felt when her eyes had met Lacey's in the principal's office. Last week Kiki had been furious: Lacey had tried to bribe her out of the race for Peach Blossom Queen. Lacey didn't give a hoot for anyone but herself. She could be the biggest witch at Paradiso High. But Lacey was also outrageous and fun, and if she thought the world revolved around her, maybe it was because when Lacey was in a room, it seemed as if it really did. Until last week, Lacey had been Kiki's best friend. If she hadn't been so angry, Kiki

71

might have missed Lacey. Losing April was enough. Kiki turned away from the sketch of the Pinks and looked at the rest of April's work.

Mr. Woolery closed his eyes. "It's so unfair. So damned unfair." His voice sounded close to cracking. "She was so gifted. She had such a wonderful eye. And soul." He opened his eyes and looked at Kiki. "She was—well, she was more than just another student to me."

Kiki didn't know what to say. Mr. Woolery was so intense. So shaken by April's death. What was he trying to tell her? How deep were his feelings for April? And then there was April's drawing of him.

An unwanted thought came into Kiki's head. Everyone had heard the gossip that had gone around school about April. How she couldn't say no to any guy—and didn't want to. Kiki banished the ugly thought. That rumor had gotten started because April had drunk too much at a party at Lacey's house and been talked into playing strip poker. April had felt miserable about it afterward.

Kiki studied Mr. Woolery. No. He was just trying to tell her that April had been his friend. Besides, Mr. Woolery was a *teacher*. Sure, some of the kids called him Mark. And plenty of the girls at school had crushes on him. It seemed that with Mr. Woolery's arrival at Paradiso High, every girl had become interested in art. But he knew what was right for a teacher and what wasn't. Didn't he?

Mr. Woolery put down the sketch he was holding and got to his feet. He came over to where Kiki was standing and put a hand on her shoulder. "So. What can I do for you anyway, Kiki?" he asked.

Kiki automatically found herself taking a step away from Mr. Woolery, and instantly she felt bad. He was terribly upset. Kiki could relate to that. "Well, I guess I came in here to work on my painting. April gave me some suggestions. I thought— well, that it would be a nice way of remembering her."

"I'm touched," Mr. Woolery said. "I was just trying to come up with a good way of remembering her myself. I thought maybe I'd try to put on an exhibit of her work."

Kiki nodded. "That's a good idea."

"So," Mr. Woolery said. He shifted from one foot to the other. "Oh, I guess you can't really do your work with all the easels and stuff pushed out of the way."

"It's okay," Kiki said. "I'll do it some other time."

"No, I'd be happy to set you up," Mr. Woolery insisted. "I have to put the room back together for my next class anyway."

Kiki glanced at the clock on the wall at the front

of the room. "Well, lunch is almost over. I think I'll work on it later."

Kiki wasn't all that eager to sit in the art room with Mr. Woolery. She'd come in here to be with her memories of April. But she hadn't expected to see April's whole life spread out on the art room floor.

CHAPTER 7

The pale late afternoon light cut through the trees and cast hard-edged shadows on the dirt road. The weird shapes on the ground moved slowly and eerily in the breeze. Everything seemed extra bright because of the rain earlier that day. It was spookier than the dark, Hope thought. Or maybe everything was spooky since April's murder.

Hope felt as if everything were moving in slow motion, as if time had lost its momentum without April. She'd gone through school in a fog, dully memorizing the combination to the new locker she'd been assigned, on a different hall from her old one, going from one class to another on automatic pilot. A dark cloud separated her from everyone else at school. And then there were those all too frequent moments when the image of April's arm pierced the protection of her foggy cocoon. What did it matter if they'd changed her locker, if she didn't have to go past that spot ever again? She still continued to see it in her mind's eye. Over and over.

Hope walked down the center of the road toward Spike's. She didn't want to get too close to the trees and bushes that lined the shoulder. She knew she was being silly, but what if something jumped out at her? Or someone? But what protection was walking in the middle of the lonely road going to provide? Even at four o'clock in the afternoon, the route out to Spike's got only a very occasional car or Jeep. Hope was alone. And very much on guard.

Calm down. But she couldn't. She wished someone like Jess were here with her. Okay, not someone like him. Him. Jess himself, a strong, safe arm against her hurt and fear. Jess, Jess would make it all better.

Spike's house isn't much farther. Once she got there, she'd be okay. She had been out to Spike's one time before, with April. It wasn't much of a place. Hope knew other kids who lived in trailer homes, but the ones she'd been in were cozy and clean and well furnished. The Mendoza sisters had a porch and a lawn and flower garden out front, and there was as much room inside as there was in Hope's neat little adobe house. But Spike's wasn't like that. It looked as if the trailer had gotten a flat tire on this out-of-the-way road, and someone had limped it over to a bald patch in the trees and let it die there.

Hope was coming up on it. There was the clearing, and she could see the green and white trailer, a broken-down car junked off to one side and a satellite dish rising on the other. A scruffy little brown and white dog barked at Hope as she made her way to the trailer.

"Shhh, boy, shhh," Hope said. She let the dog sniff her hand, and when it calmed down, she patted its head. The dog followed her to the front door. Hope knocked, a hollow metallic knock. No one answered. She knocked again. Silence.

"Spike?" she called. "Anybody home?" She went over to one of the windows and peered in. Oh, God! Oh, no! Spike's mother was sprawled motionless on the floor of the trailer, one shoe on, one shoe off, her hair disheveled, her clothes in disarray.

Oh, my God, she's dead! Hope felt a hand come down on her shoulder. She heard her own scream pierce the air.

"Hope. Hope, I didn't mean to scare you."

Hope whirled around to find herself staring at Spike. There was a deep five o'clock shadow on his dark face. Something glinted in his hand—a wrench—and his hands and arms were streaked with grease. His T-shirt was dirty, and his eyes were

puffy and tired looking. With him were his two
little brothers, one of them a pint-size Spike look-
alike.

"Spike," Hope said, her voice shaking.

"I was working on my bike around back," Spike
said.

"Spike, your mother . . ." Hope said, gesturing
to the trailer window. "Is she . . ."

Spike waved the wrench in the air. "Ah, she just
had a bad afternoon at the Blue Hawaii." The Blue
Hawaii was a dive of a bar out past the truck stop
on Route 9. Hope had never been inside, but every
once in a while something would happen there that
made it into the *Record.*

"Oh," Hope said, relieved. "So. Where've you
been?"

Spike tousled one of his brothers' hair. "Why
don't you guys go ride your bikes, okay?"

They got the bicycles that lay on the ground in
front of the trailer. "Vroom-vroom!" the little one
said as they began riding down the dusty road.

"Just like big brother Spike on his Harley, huh?"
Hope remarked.

"Yeah." Spike gave a sad smile.

Then they stood there for a long time. Hope
looked down at her hands.

"I couldn't go," Spike finally said. "I couldn't
watch them put her into the ground." His voice

was low and quiet, but Spike's voice was always like that.

Hope let out a long sigh. "It was horrible."

"I figured."

"You haven't been in school, either."

"No," Spike admitted.

"I can understand," Hope said. "But Spike, at some point you're going to have to come back."

Spike shrugged. "I don't know. I don't see why. Hey. You want something to drink? I think there's tea. I could make us some iced tea."

"That's okay," Hope said. "Maybe just a glass of water. It's a long walk."

"I'll bring it out," Spike said. He disappeared into the trailer.

Hope sat down on a patch of grass. She was just as happy not to go inside and see Mrs. Navarrone looking like a dead woman and smelling like the Blue Hawaii. Spike came back out a minute later with two glasses. He handed one to Hope and sat down next to her.

"Spike, you can't get through everything but the last month of high school and then just drop out," Hope said.

Spike took a sip of water. "Oh, they'll probably pass me, this late in the year. And if they don't, so what?"

"College?" Hope said. She knew from April that

Spike hadn't applied. Not because he didn't want to go, but because he didn't think it was possible to go to college and work full-time to support his family.

"College," Spike said. The word fell like a lead weight. "April was trying to talk me into it. But now . . ."

Hope didn't say anything for a while. She was afraid she might start crying again. She took a few deep breaths and got hold of herself. "So what are you going to do?" she asked.

"There's no reason to hang around this town anymore. Maybe I'll take off."

Hope felt a startled jolt. "Just like that? Pack up and leave the place you've spent your whole life?"

Spike raised his shoulders. "Isn't that what you're going to do when you go east for school in the fall?"

Hope shook her head. "That's different. I'll be coming back for vacations. I'll have my room here. Paradiso will still be my home. Besides, what about your mom?"

Spike frowned. "More reason to go."

"And your brothers?"

Spike closed his eyes. When he opened them, he said, "Ricky's getting old enough to take care of the family. He's the same age I was when I started doing it. . . . I'll write to them. I'll send them money. And when I settle down for long enough, they'll be coming right out to be with me." Hope could hear the intensity in his voice. He loved those two little guys. But even they weren't enough to keep Spike in Paradiso.

"Where would you go?" Hope asked.

Spike shook his head. "I guess I'll just get on my bike and start riding and keep going. . . ." Then he said, "I'm glad you came by before I split. April really loved you."

Hope nodded and willed back a tear. "She really loved you too. Spike? Was there anything wrong?"

Spike looked away from Hope. "Wrong?" he said tightly.

"April had said she wanted to talk to me," Hope said. "About something important. She didn't sound too happy, either, and I thought—well, that maybe you knew about it."

Spike didn't say a word.

"Spike?"

"What makes you think I know?"

Hope sighed. "Come on," she said softly. "I didn't come over expecting anything, but hey, it's pretty obvious right this second that you're hiding something. I don't need my computer to figure that out. Spike? Look, she was going to tell me anyway."

"What difference does it make?" Spike said.

"She's gone. Dead. What could it possibly matter?"

"What could what matter?" Hope asked.

Spike toyed with his water glass. "You have to promise not to tell."

"I promise. Cross my heart and—" Hope stopped in mid-sentence. "I promise," she repeated.

"April thought she was pregnant," Spike said.

Hope gasped. "Oh, wow. It was—yours?" Spike frowned. "Oh, of course it was. I'm sorry, Spike. What were you going to do? Her parents would have ki—" Hope let out a low, long whistle. What if April was dead because Uncle Ward had found out? Or because Spike had found out and—no! That was crazy. "I don't know what to say," Hope said.

"Don't say anything," Spike said. "To anyone else, I mean. I wouldn't want April to be hurt any worse than—well, for her memory to be hurt. You know what I'm saying."

Hope nodded. All that old talk about April's reputation. It couldn't surface now. No. Hope wouldn't let it. "You can count on me, Spike. I'd be the last one to say a word."

"You know, Hope, it's so weird. When April told me she thought she was pregnant . . . well . . . I can't say I thought it was good news. One of the things that pulled us together, one of the things I thought was so great about her, was that she was gonna get out of Paradiso. She was so talented. She was smart, too. She knew something like 'Peach Blossom Queen' "—he spat the words out—"was nothing compared to what we could have someday. As soon as she told me she might be pregnant, all I could think was, *Stuck*. But now that she's gone, I think I would rather have stayed with April in Paradiso forever if I had to, than go anywhere in the world without her."

"I know what you mean," Hope said softly. "When we were in elementary school, we used to play this game where we would imagine what it would be like to be grown up. We always pretended we lived in houses side by side and still did everything together, but were just a little more grown up. Except instead of homework and dolls, we'd get married, go shopping, go to work. When we got older, we started to realize it probably wouldn't happen that way, but I never thought it would end because of something like this. I miss her so much."

"Yeah," said Spike. "Me too. He turned his head away. When he turned back, he said, "Listen, Hope, do you think you could do me one more favor? I need someone to get my stuff from my locker at school before I leave. I just can't face going in there."

"I really can't talk you out of leaving?" Hope asked.

Spike shook his head. "Not now. At first, I thought I'd stay. Try to find the bastard who did this." His voice rose. "Then he'd be gone. History!"

Crash! Spike hurled his glass at the front of the trailer. The sound of glass on metal rang out as it shattered into pieces, catching the sun so that it looked like an explosion.

Hope gave a startled cry. From inside the trailer, Mrs. Navarrone let out a hung-over moan.

"Sorry," Spike said. He let out a breath. "See, that's why I have to go away."

"Spike, you've got to let the law take care of justice," Hope said.

He looked at her. "You really believe that? My dad's doing time for some other dude's crime." He shrugged. "Anyway, if I stayed around here, I'd probably end up in jail with him."

Hope heard Spike's mother moving around inside the trailer. It was time for her to go. "Spike," she pleaded one last time. "Don't run away. My dad did, and it only messes everything up worse. I know."

Spike looked Hope straight in the eye. "My mind is made up, Hope. There's no changing it. I'm outta here. I'm counting on you to get my stuff before I split." His little brothers came up the road on their bikes. He followed them with his eyes. "As hard as it's going to be to leave."

When she thought about it, Hope could understand why Spike needed to run away. What she didn't understand, though, was what exactly he was running from.

CHAPTER 8

Raven spotted trouble walking in the door of Rosa's Café. Actually, she saw it pulling up in a long, black limousine first. Only one person owned a limo like that in Paradiso. And unless someone had taken a way-wrong turn out of Beverly Hills, Calvin Pinkerton was making a call.

Raven served up a *quesadilla* supreme to John Mattinsky, Doug's father, at a corner table and raced back to the papers she had left on the counter. She was hiding the pages of her Stop the Greenway Mall petition under the coffee machine when Lacey's father walked in. And Lacey's mother, too.

As far as Raven knew, Mr. and Mrs. Pinkerton had never set foot in Rosa's before. And for good reason. Back before Raven was born, Cal Pinkerton had fired Manny Cruz for trying to organize the workers at Pinkerton Canneries for better benefits. He had said it was for stealing, but Manuel Cruz had never done anything more dishonest than telling his kids there was a Santa Claus.

Raven wanted to ask the Pinkertons if perhaps they didn't feel a little overdressed for Rosa's. Mr. Pinkerton had on a white linen suit and a straw Panama hat, and Mrs. Pinkerton was done up in some red thing that poufed in the middle and made her look like a tulip and her infamous sunglasses, which she didn't take off even inside.

Some people had all the money in the world for expensive clothes, but the poor things were born without a molecule of taste, Raven thought. She wondered if she should tell them to get out. For Papa. Then she reconsidered. Papa would do it on principle. But why not serve the Pinkertons and put their dollars in the cash register? They certainly had enough, and with Mama's doctor bills, the Cruzes could use all the business they could get.

"Good afternoon, young lady," Calvin Pinkerton said, slipping on his best smile and putting his hat on the counter.

"Good afternoon," Raven said suspiciously. That hat looked as if it belonged at some English lawn party. Where did Calvin Pinkerton think he was?

Mr. Pinkerton sat down on one of the stools at the long Formica counter. "Come, dear, have a seat," he said to his wife. Raven saw her cast a dubious look at the stool next to him, as if it might not be good enough for her precious behind. She sat down as if the seat were sticky, her mouth curled into a look of distaste.

"I'll have a cup of coffee," Mr. Pinkerton said. "And some of that pudding." He pointed to the top shelf of the dessert cooler behind the counter.

"Flan," Raven corrected. She looked at Mrs. Pinkerton.

"Nothing for me," Mrs. Pinkerton said. Probably thinks she's too good to drink out of our cups, Raven thought. When she looked at Darla Pinkerton, Raven could see Lacey in twenty or thirty years —a bitter, nasty witch with an attitude to cover up for all the disappointments in her life. Mrs. Pinkerton was probably furious that Lacey had lost the Peach Blossom contest.

Raven filled a cup with coffee and set it down in front of Calvin Pinkerton. "Thank you, young lady," he said. "Raven, isn't it?"

"Yes," Raven said coolly. The one who's going to run your mall out of town, and you know it, she thought. She served him a dish of flan from the dessert cooler.

"I hear you want to go to college," he said.

"I *am* going to college," Raven answered. What

was Calvin Pinkerton's game? He couldn't just be making conversation. Not when he knew Raven was doing everything she could to stop his plans for the mall. She wondered if he had looked out the limo window at the scrublands that stretched behind the diner. Did he see anything but dollar signs in the wild, unspoiled beauty?

"The way I hear it," Calvin Pinkerton said, "you have your heart set on one very special school. Special and expensive, I might add."

Raven had to restrain herself from tipping Mr. Pinkerton's hot coffee into his lap. The nerve of him! And he said it so calmly, so agreeably, as if he were making small talk about the weather.

"I've gotten into three very good schools," Raven said tightly. "Now, if you'll excuse me, I have other customers to wait on."

"But you want to go to Stanford," Cal Pinkerton went on, not letting Raven get away.

Damn you, Lacey Pinkerton! Raven thought. She balled her fists inside the pockets of her white apron. What was Lacey, Daddy's little spy? Did he get his information by giving her weekly bonuses on her allowance? Raven was sure Lacey had told him the rest of the story too. That unless Stanford offered Raven more scholarship money, she was going to have to go to one of her second-choice schools.

Was that what Calvin Pinkerton was driving at? Bribe money? Raven felt her head spinning.

Calvin Pinkerton confirmed her suspicions. "Well, young lady, what if I said I could help?" He took a bite of flan. "Mmm, very good." The man was without shame. "Think of it as a kind of local scholarship. I feel it's my responsibility to help the community, much as you might not think so."

Raven had been brought up to be polite to adults. But she couldn't hold her tongue a moment longer. "Mr. Pinkerton," she said, "the only responsibility you feel is to your wallet."

"Well, I never!" declared Darla Pinkerton icily. "You make a generous offer to this—this—"

"This nobody?" Raven suggested.

"No one's calling you that," Mr. Pinkerton cut in smoothly. "My wife is just trying to say that you shouldn't be so quick to refuse my little gift. Think of me as a kind of uncle, interested in your education. You know, *I* do have the best interests of the people of Paradiso in mind. The Greenway Mall, for example. It will be a good, safe place for our citizens, a boon to our town economy, a step toward modernization . . ."

Raven's temper was as hot as a bottle of chili sauce. "I don't have anything to say to you, Mr. Pinkerton." She turned on the heel of her sneakers and went over to the windows at the end of the counter. The Pinkertons' chauffeur had gotten out of the car and was throwing a ball to Raven's littlest brother. Through the open window Raven could hear him encouraging her brother in Spanish.

"That's it, little guy. Here, try again."

Behind them, the scrublands stretched out in the warm glow of late afternoon. Grasses rippled with the patterns of the wind. The low trees and bushes that grew close together were home to all kinds of birds and animals. To destroy them was tantamount to—murder. Raven's thoughts went to April. Why anyone would want to kill her was a far bigger mystery than why Cal Pinkerton and Lars Cutter wanted to destroy the scrublands. Raven had just that afternoon heard a new rumor about Jess Gardner: he'd been seen driving in town with April the night of the murder. Raven didn't want to believe that Vaughn's best friend could have had anything to do with April's death. But *somebody* killed April, she reminded herself.

Out of the corner of her eye, Raven saw the Pinkertons getting up to leave. Calvin Pinkerton put on his lawn-party hat. Darla Pinkerton marched straight to the door as if the air in Rosa's wasn't an expensive enough brand for her to breathe. Before leaving the café, Calvin Pinkerton came over to Raven and pressed a crisp, green bill into her palm.

"This ought to cover my coffee and that pudding," he said.

Raven looked down at her hand. She held a one-hundred-dollar bill!

"Don't have anything smaller," Mr. Pinkerton said. "Keep the change. And just think about my offer." He turned and walked out of the restaurant, his step smugly confident.

Raven stared at the money. No way! She wasn't going to let him pull a stunt like this. She ran after him, wadding up the bill. But before she got to the door, she stopped. She uncurled her fist and looked at the balled-up money. She opened it up and smoothed it out. It could pay for her mama's entire doctor bill and her prescription at the pharmacy, too.

Raven glanced at Mr. Mattinsky. He had his nose stuck in the pages of the *Record*. The two truck drivers at the other end of the counter weren't paying much attention either. Raven knew what Papa would say. "That money—it's *el diablo*. The devil."

Raven sank into a chair at an empty table and put her head down on the cool red-and-white-checked tablecloth. Calvin Pinkerton's money was going to go toward something important for once. And Raven certainly didn't intend to be bought off on the mall. She heard the Pinkertons' limousine pulling away. She would put the hundred dollars in the cash register, but she wouldn't tell Papa where it had come from.

Some mysteries were better left unsolved.

CHAPTER 9

It was dark by the time Spike dropped Hope off on Old Town Road. The Big Dipper hung over Paradiso, and Hope felt as if it were pouring down a nasty potion of misery and fear.

"You sure you don't want me to take you the rest of the way home?" Spike asked as Hope handed him her helmet.

Hope shook her head, her long dark hair swirling around her shoulders. It felt good to take the heavy helmet off. "Thanks, but I've got to get some stuff in town, and I need to walk a little. Think about—everything." Hope didn't want to add that being on the back of Spike's motorcycle scared her. Spike was not the kind of guy who drove slowly, and she was happy have gotten off his bike in one piece.

"Okay," Spike said. "You'll bring me the things in my locker tomorrow?"

"After school," Hope said.

"Thanks. I really appreciate it." He scribbled his combination on the back of a gum wrapper he'd fished from his pocket and handed it to her.

"No problem." It was the least she could do for someone who had been so special to April. Hope watched Spike roar off in a cloud of exhaust. She felt so tired, as if the day had gone on for a week. Tired and unbearably sad. Poor Spike. Poor April. Hope let out a noisy breath as she trudged down Old Town Road. *Poor me.*

She felt extra burdened by the news of April's pregnancy. Her cousin's last days must have been filled with worry and tension. Plus it made Hope feel as if two murders had been committed at once. On the way out to Spike's she hadn't thought she could feel any worse. But she felt worse. Spike had dumped this huge secret on her, and now he was going to take off. There wouldn't even be anybody for her to talk to about it.

But what would you say about it anyway? Hope asked herself. That April would have been a happy mother? No. April had plans for herself, for her art. Getting pregnant had definitely not been in the plans. That her parents would have been supportive of whatever decision she had made? No way. Uncle Ward and Aunt Sara probably would have locked April up in a convent for the rest of her life. There was just no point in even thinking about it. It was over. Over and dead.

Hope stepped farther to the side of Old Town Road as headlights signaled an approaching car. Behind it was another one. The first car whizzed past her, but the second car was slowing down. Hope looked around. No one else was in sight. The headlights were getting closer—and the car was braking to a stop.

Hope's breath caught in her throat. She wanted to run, but her feet were frozen. The car pulled up alongside her. As it caught the beam of a streetlight, Hope saw it was a vintage shiny red Pontiac. Jess! Her terror fizzled away, but her pulse kept right on racing.

Jess leaned across the passenger's seat and rolled down the window. "Hope! I thought you might want a ride." Hope could feel Jess looking at her. "Or maybe a little cheering up," he added.

Suddenly Hope didn't feel like walking anymore. "You're right," she said shyly.

Jess unlocked the door for her, and she slid in.

"Where're you headed?" Jess asked.

"Town. I need a couple of things before the stores close."

He nodded. "Can I drop you at the turnoff to the garage? Dad's not there right now, and we've got a customer coming for his car, and I've still got to put in a new set of spark plugs for him." Jess patted a paper bag in between them on the seat. "I had to drive out to San Pedro to get them."

Hope looked at the paper bag. She wouldn't know a spark plug if she tripped over it. Maybe it was dumb to think Jess could ever be interested in her. She nodded, feeling a little uncomfortable.

"So. You looked pretty down when I stopped," Jess commented.

Hope nodded again.

"Yeah, me too," Jess said. He steered around a curve. "It's really hard. I can't get myself to stop thinking about April."

"Yeah," Hope said. "I'll manage to get something else in my head—just for a few seconds—and then . . . all of a sudden that picture pops into my mind. . . ."

"I know." Jess blew out a long breath. "In swim practice today I was in the middle of a lap and— well, you know."

"Yeah, I do."

"I got out of the pool and left. I just couldn't concentrate. Wow, but listen to me going on. I'm really sorry, Hope. This must be so much worse for you." They drove by the Blue Belle Dairy, lit up for business. "You were so close to her. You and Spike."

Yeah, me and Spike, Hope thought. Only he's going to run away and leave me to deal with

Paradiso and this whole horrible thing. Then she felt bad. She could understand why Spike would want to leave Paradiso far behind. One day of school had made Hope want to shut herself up in her room with her computer and not come out again.

"Where's Spike been, anyway?" Jess asked. "I haven't seen his Harley around."

"Actually, I was just coming from visiting him," Hope admitted. "He didn't come to school today." She didn't add that he was planning on leaving Paradiso—or that he'd told her a shocking secret about April. She wished she could. Boy, it would feel so good to be able to share it with someone. But she had promised. And how well did she really know Jess Gardner, anyway? Not that she wouldn't like to know him better. She sneaked a look at his handsome face, so serious right now under a mop of thick, wavy reddish-blond hair, his strong swimmer's arms reaching to the steering wheel. He looked over for a moment and smiled. Hope felt a tingle of warmth.

"So how is Spike?" Jess asked.

"Not so hot," Hope said. "He's pretty wrecked by . . . what happened." She wanted to tell Jess so badly!

"Yeah, dumb question," Jess said. If he noticed Hope was holding something back, it didn't show.

"From what I've heard, you're a genius with anything mechanical," Hope said.

"Well, cars and lawn mowers and washing machines," Jess said. "Things like that. But not computers. Those kinds of machines are more for the brilliant types like you."

Hope laughed. "A computer isn't really a machine. It's more like a person."

Jess raised an eyebrow. "Yeah? How do you figure that?"

"Well," Hope explained, "people, human beings like you and me, write the programs you use on a computer, right? So if you can figure out the way someone was thinking when they designed a particular program, it's pretty easy to learn to use it."

"I don't know," Jess said.

"I do," Hope said. Computers were the one thing she had real confidence about. "On the other hand, if you pulled a muffler out of that bag and told me it was a spark plug, I wouldn't know the difference."

Jess laughed. "Hope, a muffler wouldn't come close to fitting in that bag."

"See what I mean?" said Hope.

"Look, I have an idea," Jess said. "What if you come back to the garage with me, and I'll show you how to change a set of spark plugs? After Huck Spector picks up his car, I'll run you into town."

Hope felt herself smile. Something was actually going right today. "Sure. I'd like that," she said.

"Great," Jess responded. He made a turn down Division Lane. "And then maybe some other time, you can give me some pointers in the computer room," he added.

Hope felt her smile get bigger.

"That was really cool the way you set up that computer betting program for the Peach Blossom Queen contest," Jess said.

Peach Blossom Queen. April. Hope felt the smile slip off her face.

"Whoa, I'm really sorry," Jess said.

"No." Hope shook her head. "Don't be. I mean, we have to just start trying to get used to the fact that she's not here anymore."

"Yeah," Jess said softly.

"Jess, I've been meaning to tell you, I really appreciated you being there for me that day. I mean, I don't know what I would have done if I'd been by myself."

Jess reached over and touched Hope's shoulder for a moment. "Hey," he said. "I wish you hadn't needed me. But I guess it's a good thing I happened to be there."

Happened to be there . . . Jess's hand still on her shoulder, Hope couldn't stop a brutal thought from crossing her mind. What *had* Jess been doing near Hope's locker anyway? His own locker was on another hall. Then Hope took in the concern in Jess's blue eyes and she immediately felt guilty at her own thought. Where did *that* come from? Jess was too nice to hurt a soul. And too handsome . . .

He put his hand back on the steering wheel and pulled into the driveway of Gardner's Auto Body and Repair. "Well, here we are."

Hope unhooked her seat belt and let herself out of the car. Gardner's was a large, low, cement-block garage, surrounded by a lot on three sides. Cars of all kinds were parked in an orderly fashion around the building. The inside smelled of grease and gasoline. Jess flipped on the lights. There were tools and machines in every available bit of space. In one corner was a deep green Volkswagen Karmann Ghia in perfect condition.

"Beauty, isn't it?" Jess said. "It would be fun to go for a spin in it, huh?"

"Yeah," Hope answered. With you, it would be fun to go for a spin in any car, she thought. She turned her face away from him, hoping he wouldn't see her blush.

"And that tan Ford over there?" Jess said. "That's Huck Spector's car. All set to go except for the spark plugs that you're going to put in."

"Me? Wait a second," Hope protested.

Jess grinned. "Hope, you can change a light bulb, right?"

"Well, yeah, sure."

"Okay." He went over to the Ford and opened the hood. Hope followed him and peered inside. All she saw were a bunch of grimy pipes and tubes connecting a bunch of mysterious boxes and bottles.

"And this," said Jess, taking a cylindrical ceramic and metal plug from the paper bag he'd had on the car seat, "is a spark plug."

Hope stared at the spark plug, then back under the hood of the car. "Jess, you know I could solve an equation for how that spark plug works—assuming you put the problem in front of me on my computer screen. But I could look in here all week and I couldn't figure out where to put that thing."

Jess laughed. "And I'm just the opposite. I could build a car engine in my sleep. But equations?" He reached under the hood and patted the biggest, grimiest box. "I have to be able to reach out and touch something to know how it works. Now this— this is the engine. And look." Jess grabbed hold of a small circle of metal sticking up from the engine. "Presto!" He pulled loose a cylinder just like the one he'd taken from the bag.

"That's all?" Hope asked. "You pull the old one out and put the new one in?"

Jess nodded. "You know that kid's toy where you have to put the square peg in the square hole and the round one in the round hole?" They both laughed. "I told you it was simple," he said. He handed her another new spark plug from the brown paper bag. "Here. Why don't you try replacing the one next to the one I just did?"

Hope grabbed hold of the next old spark plug and pulled. She felt it give way. "Blast off!" she said. She eased the new spark plug in until she felt it click into place.

"Pretty good for someone who walks everywhere," Jess remarked. "Wanna do the other four?" He held the brown paper bag out toward her, and as his hand brushed hers, Hope felt a different kind of spark.

She looked up at Jess. His eyes were so blue. Then, shyly, she looked away, fumbling a little as she started to change the remaining spark plugs. She could feel Jess right behind her as she worked. He was so close to her. She handed him the old spark plugs one by one as she removed them from the car. Her fingertips touched his hand each time, and she could feel herself trembling.

As she turned to him and put the last spark plug in his palm, he closed his fingers around her hand, holding it gently. "You've got grease all over your hands," he said softly. Hope looked down at their intertwined hands, holding the last dirty old spark plug. Then she looked up at Jess. He wasn't looking at her hands. He was looking right into her eyes. His gaze held hers. Hope felt her heart pounding so hard she thought Jess must be able to hear it.

She gave a start as a man's voice echoed in the garage. "Hello?" came his greeting from the entrance to the shop. Hope and Jess dropped hands. Huck Spector, the barber.

"There's a specter haunting Paradiso," Jess joked softly to Hope. Then he turned toward the barber. "Hi, Mr. Spector," he said more loudly. "We were just finishing up work on your car."

"New assistant?" Huck Spector asked. He looked at Hope. Hope opened her mouth, but Jess answered first. "Right, Mr. Spector. Computer genius and auto mechanic in training."

Huck Spector nodded. "Lucky boy, Jess." Jess just grinned. Hope was sure she was turning as red as a stop sign.

Huck Spector took care of his bill, and Jess gave him back the keys to his car. "Thank you, my boy," Huck said. "And stop by some afternoon. Your hair's getting a little long."

Hope loved the way Jess's hair curled around his collar, but she didn't say anything.

Huck Spector got into the Ford and started the motor. As he pulled out of the garage he stuck his head out the window. "Ah, Miss Hubbard?" he said. "I'm very sorry about your cousin."

Hope felt the magic of the past few minutes die. Her mind filled with a picture of April's cold body. "Thank you," she managed to say. She swallowed hard as he drove away.

"Hope," Jess said, as soon as they were alone again. "Are you all right?"

She nodded. "I guess. I'd finally stopped thinking about her for a few minutes."

"Me too," Jess said. Then he added, "Listen, come by whenever you want, if it helps."

Hope felt a small smile returning to her face. "Okay."

"So . . ." Jess said.

"So . . ." Hope repeated.

"I suppose I should get you into town before everything closes," Jess said.

"I suppose," Hope said. But the computer paper and the jar of honey she needed to buy didn't seem very important right now. She wished Jess would ask her to stay and help him with something else. Instead, he turned off the garage lights and locked up after them.

Hope followed Jess out to his car and tried not to feel too disappointed.

CHAPTER 10

OPENING REAL SOON. WE CAN HARDLY WAIT. HOPE YOU CAN'T EITHER. Lacey read the notice spotlighted in the shop window. A slew of carpenters, electricians, and painters were working overtime to get the new store ready for business. Paradiso would soon have its first exclusive women's boutique.

Lacey and Penny sat on the grass at the edge of the town green sipping sodas and trying to find the brightest star in the sky. At least Penny was trying. Lacey was more interested in the handsome sign painter across the street. In the light of a street lamp she watched him put the finishing touches on a fancy wooden plaque that was hanging outside the store.

"The Virginia Shop of Beverly Hills," she read out loud. "Can you believe it, Penny? Little ole

Paradiso's hitting the big time. Pretty stupid idea, don't you think?"

Penny came back to earth. "How come, Lacey? It looks cool."

"Yeah, but who's kidding who? Daddy's mall project is only a matter of time. Why would anybody start a business downtown when it's gonna become a ghost town?"

"Yeah, you're probably right, Lacey," Penny agreed.

"The next sign he'll be painting will be 'Going Out of Business Sale.' Well, at least he's cute. I wouldn't mind watching him paint signs forever." Lacey laughed as she looked around at the other businesses that were also on their last leg. Huck Spector's barbershop for one, which stuck out like a sore thumb, a little brick box sandwiched in between Paradiso's two giants, the Pinkerton Building and Vaughn Cutter's father's bank, Cutter Savings and Loan.

She spotted Lars Cutter outside his bank with some maintenance workers. The bank, a huge, white, windowless structure, was a prime target for graffiti. She watched the workers scrubbing away the day's comments on April's murder, all lit up by the flood of night lights that bathed the walls of the building.

She read the words out loud, dramatizing them

as if she were a TV soap opera actress. " 'Who killed April? Was it May, or June? Or could it be you? Poor Peggy Sue.' "

Lacey laughed, but Penny was silent. "Hey, come on, Penny, I'm just kidding around. Besides, look at that picture underneath. It's a riot."

Underneath the lettering was a picture of a girl wearing a diamond-studded crown. In one hand she held a rope and in the other a paintbrush. There was a caption scribbled next to it that read *Queen for a day*.

"Whoever did that picture must have some sick sense of humor," Penny said, making a gagging motion with her tongue for emphasis. "It's gross!"

"I'll bet it was Eddie Hagenspitzel," Lacey said. "That's his line. Definitely."

Lacey took a big gulp of her soda and sighed. "I'll tell you one thing. It'll be a lot easier to find the graffiti artist than the murderer."

"Maybe, but it looks like they're getting close," Penny said.

Lacey let out a raw laugh. "What? You mean that stuff about Jess?" But she felt her heart skip a beat.

"Well . . ." Penny said coyly.

Lacey rolled her eyes. "Come on, Penny, you don't really believe that garbage. Jess Gardner a killer? He used to be in the church choir. In third grade he was a Cub Scout. And remember last year when he refused to do the biology lab? Jess couldn't even kill an earthworm, and now you're telling me he's a murderer. No way. Besides, why would he want to kill April?"

"Well, Janice Campbell told me that Doug Mattinsky was telling Renée that Jess was nervous the sheriff might find out and come after him."

"Let's see now, Pen. I heard it from you, and you found out from Janice, who heard from Renée being told by Doug, who heard from Jess. Does that make it fourth- or fifth-hand information? Seems like yet one more rumor from the Paradiso High Gossip Club to me."

"There's more. But no one knows about it, Lacey." Penny paused. "I'll tell you. But I'm warning you, it looks bad."

"Come on, Pen, out with it," Lacey demanded. "You're starting to make me nervous."

Penny took a deep breath. "Well, last week when I was working in my dad's store, Jess came in and bought something . . . he bought a wrench and some nylon cord. I didn't think anything of it at first, but after talking to him today and hearing what he said to Doug, well . . ."

"I don't believe it," Lacey blurted. "I just don't buy it."

Penny looked shaken. "You don't think I'm lying, do you, Lacey?"

"No, Penny, not you. I just know Jess wouldn't kill anyone. Simply not the type. Too nice, you know?" Lacey felt her stomach start to calm down a bit as her own words convinced her of Jess's innocence. "Yeah, you had me there for a minute, Pen. I guess all that evidence could make a pretty good case. But I know Jess better than anyone."

With a bit of hesitation, Penny nodded. "Yeah, you're probably right, Lacey." She tugged at the grass in frustration. "Anyway, I'm sick of hearing about 'poor April.' Everybody's acting as if she had just won Queen of the World instead of Peach Blossom Queen—which she robbed from you anyway. And this business about a murderer on the loose is so silly. If you ask me, it's totally possible that April was Paradiso's first and last murder of the year. I mean, maybe somebody just couldn't stand her. Simple as that."

Lacey was chewing on Penny's own special and strange brand of logic when she heard a familiar roar in the distance. "Speak of the devil," she said as the sound of Jess's GTO, revving up at 6000 rpm, grew louder. "Hey! I know that sound anywhere. Here comes your lady killer now."

"Maybe the news is out and he's making his getaway!" Penny exclaimed.

"Penny, you've got the world's biggest imagination! And you obviously don't know Jess the way I do."

For a moment Lacey let her thoughts wander and get lost in the past. A vision of her arms wrapped tightly around Jess came to her, and she felt a warm tingling all over. And Jess whispering in Lacey's ear how much he loved her. They were wild about each other.

Only then her thoughts turned to the whole mess over Jess and Michelle Wheeler—the mess that caused their breakup—and her dreamy smile turned sour. She remembered the night Jess had canceled their date at the last minute, leaving Lacey home alone on a weekend night. She was decked out in a brand-new miniskirt waiting for him. "I can't tell you; I just gotta cancel. It's an emergency. I'll see you in school on Monday. Okay?" Click.

It wasn't okay, damn it! When Lacey found out that Jess had been seen driving around with Michelle Wheeler on that fateful night, there was no other choice but to break up with him. Later, Jess swore he was only helping Michelle out in an emergency. He swore to Lacey there was nothing between Michelle and him. But he still wouldn't tell her what Michelle needed him for. *Then I won't take you back, Jess. No way.* Even as she said them,

Lacey thought she would regret those words one day.

Lacey had only recently found out through the grapevine that Michelle had been pregnant and that her boyfriend had split when he found out. Michelle had needed Jess's help to get to a doctor.

Maybe I was too hard on him, she thought. Yeah. He's really an honest guy. I think he does deserve a second chance. And there's no time like the present. Lacey felt her mood pick up as she waited for him to appear.

"What's taking him so long, Lacey?" Penny asked. "Are you sure that's Jess's car coming?"

"Huh?" Penny had startled Lacey. "Sorry, Pen. I was spacing out for a sec. Yeah, that's him." She pointed to his red GTO as it pulled around the corner into view under a streetlight. "Check it out —there he is."

The car came to a halt on the corner in front of Radio Shack.

"Come on, Penny. Let's go say hi."

"I don't know, Lacey. He might be dangerous." Penny looked nervous. "What if—"

Lacey cut her off. "Oh, Penny. You're getting as good at believing rumors as you are at starting them. Never mind, I'll go myself."

Then, noting Penny's crestfallen expression, she paused long enough to give Penny's shoulder a reassuring squeeze. "Hey, I know you're just looking out for me. But don't worry, I can handle this."

Though she didn't like to admit it, the truth was that Lacey depended on Penny's big mouth more than Penny realized. When she cooked up a rumor to get back at someone, Lacey had Penny to do her dirty work and could keep her own nose clean. But if she didn't put Penny down once in a while, keep her in her place, Penny might get a swelled head. And as far as Lacey was concerned, the Pinks had room for only one queen bee . . . and she was it.

As Lacey started across the street she noticed someone in the passenger seat of Jess's car. Who's that with him? she wondered. She kept her distance. It was dark, but she could tell from the little bit of light shining into the car from the street that he was with a girl. Lacey felt her good mood do a nosedive. She watched Jess get out of his car and hop around to the passenger's side to let the girl out. Suddenly she felt better. Phew, it's just Hope Hubbard. Lacey was relieved.

"Jess!" Lacey called. "Hey, gorgeous!"

But he didn't hear her. She started toward him but stopped dead in her tracks when she saw something that totally blew her mind. Jess Gardner, the most handsome guy in town, took Hope's hand in his. Lacey's mouth dropped open as she saw Jess move his other hand gently across Hope's cheek.

They smiled at each other, and then Hope turned and headed for Radio Shack.

"C'mon!" Lacey cried to Penny as she barrelled toward Jess's car.

She grabbed the door just as Jess was shifting into gear. "Well, hello," she said, peering into the car. Jess practically rocketed through the ceiling at the sound of her voice. She knew she had to move fast. "A little on edge these days?" she purred. "I can understand why. All those ridiculous rumors flying around. I just wanted to tell you, I don't believe any of it."

Some of the tension ebbed from Jess's face and body. "Really?" he said. "Thanks, Lace. You're one of the few."

Lacey leaned a little closer to him. "Don't forget how well I know you. Better than just about anybody. If you need me, I'm here for you." Before Jess could object, Lacey grabbed his face with her hands and gave him a nice, long kiss.

When she moved away again, Jess sat there for a minute, a look of surprise mingled with a big dose of satisfaction on his face. "What you are, Lacey," he finally said, "is trouble." Sliding the stick shift smoothly into first gear, he roared away.

All of a sudden Penny tapped Lacey on the shoulder, giving her a start. "Check it out, Lacey. Look who just saw the whole thing."

They went over to where Hope was standing.

Lacey and Penny positioned themselves in between Hope and the front door of Radio Shack. "Hi, Hope. How's everything?" Lacey said, her words dripping with niceness.

"What's new, Hope?" asked Penny. "Been tutoring Jess in math? I thought he already knew how to add and subtract."

"I'm sure he does. Look, I'm in a rush, so . . ." Hope started toward the store front.

But Lacey wouldn't budge. "You start your computer dating service again? Who did you match Jess up with this time? You know, it's been a while for him. He's desperate, Hope. He'd probably take anyone."

"Why don't you guys back off?" Hope asked quietly.

Lacey could tell from the slight quaver in her voice and the over-brightness of her eyes that Hope was struggling to keep from crying. She really does care about him, Lacey thought, her triumph soured by a sudden dose of envy. And he obviously cares about her . . . or why didn't he kiss me back? But what does she have that I don't? How could he possibly want her when he could have me?

"Aren't you being a bit brave riding around with Jess Gardner?" Penny persisted. "Or are you following in your cousin's footsteps?"

"Huh? What are you talking about?" Hope, her cheeks pinched with color, her face desolate, looked as if she'd forgotten all about April's murder. But now she jerked as if she'd been slapped.

Good for Penny, Lacey thought.

"You mean you don't know?" Penny continued. "You really ought to get out of the computer lab a little more often. Jess is the number one suspect in April's murder."

"Gimme a break." Hope laughed.

"It's true," Lacey said with a smirk. "The facts are out that April was last seen driving in Jess's car only two hours before the murder. And the wrench—"

"What wrench?" Hope interrupted.

Lacey enjoyed the nervous expression on Hope's face.

"The wrench that he bought from my father's hardware store. The one I sold him myself just last week," Penny said.

"Guess you'll have to tutor him in jail, Hope," Lacey needled.

"Jail? What are you saying? I don't believe it for a second," Hope said. "And the wrench doesn't mean a thing. How many did you sell last week, Penny? You think he's the only one in Paradiso with a wrench?"

"The nylon rope that he bought with it sure does

make it interesting, don't you think?" Penny added. "I think the credit card receipt will be proof enough for the sheriff. My dad's probably showing it to him now. History repeats itself. First Michelle Wheeler, now April. At least Jess didn't kill Michelle."

Hope was speechless. Lacey could tell by the blank expression on her face that Hope's vision of Jess was beginning to change.

"For your own good, Hope," Lacey said, placing an arm on Hope's shoulder, "I'd keep my distance if I were you."

"You're not me! Thank goodness for that." Hope stepped away. "Don't you two have anything better to do than hang out on street corners at night, trashing everyone in sight? You guys can be such jerks!"

Lacey contentedly watched as Hope, shaking like a leaf, brushed past Penny and went into Radio Shack.

"That'll make her think twice about getting involved with Jess. Thanks, Penny," Lacey said, slapping her a high-five. "You're always looking out for me. You're a true blue—I mean a true Pink—friend. I know I can always count on you."

Of course, as she'd protested to Penny earlier, *she* didn't believe Jess was a killer. But it didn't hurt to make Hope think twice about her new heartthrob, now did it?

Penny smiled. "No problem, Lacey. I know you still like Jess. But I really did sell him the wrench and rope."

"Yeah, well, I don't think Hope's gonna take any chances with him now. But I just might."

They both laughed. "The Pinks strike again!" Penny raised a triumphant fist in the air.

"Hey, Penny. You want a ride home?" Lacey asked. "It's no problem. We could stop by the Blue Belle Dairy and get a sundae. My treat."

"Can't. I gotta work for my dad. He's open late twice a week now. At least he pays me." She looked at her watch. "Oops. Gotta split, Lacey. Later. And watch out for Jess. You never know."

"Later, babe. See you tomorrow." Lacey watched Penny hustle down the street to Bolton's Hardware.

She hopped in her Ferrari and took off into the night at full speed. The top was down, and the breeze against her face felt great. But as she turned up Winding Hill Road and headed for home, she felt confused.

Jess, a murder suspect? It's insane!

Lacey wondered how well she really knew Jess. She thought of the ugly rumors that had started flying around about how Michelle Wheeler's out-of-town boyfriend was really just a hoax. People were saying that Jess was the real father! She shivered at the thought. But what if it were true? What if Jess was the real father? And what if he *is* April's murderer? But I think I still love him! And now that Raven and Vaughn are a real couple, I sure could use someone like Jess. . . .

Her thoughts suddenly switched to Vaughn. How could Vaughn leave me? He has some nerve. He's the first guy to ever do that to me. Am I losing my style or something? No way. He's not worth worrying about anyway. Raven can keep him for all I care.

As she pulled into her driveway her thoughts were racing all over the place. First to Vaughn. We just weren't right for each other. Then to Jess. Mmmmm. I can feel him now. Kissing me. Hugging me.

She was still in a fog as she got out of the car. But as she walked up the pathway to the house, she was brought back to reality by a frightening sight. She froze as she looked up at a tall, dark figure at the front door. With a freshly poured drink in his hand, Calvin Pinkerton was awaiting his daughter's arrival.

Lacey shook. Oh, no, please! Please don't be drunk, Daddy!

CHAPTER 11

The first thing Hope did the next morning was turn on her computer. She stared at the screen. The murderer could be anyone. April's killer was free as a bird, and Hope was getting desperate. She had made one list of everyone who had placed bets on the Peach Blossom Queen contest and another list of April's neighbors. She'd entered the sheriff's three clues: nylon rope, blunt instrument, and man's sneaker print. None of the information got Hope anywhere.

She watched the cursor on her computer screen blinking away minute after empty minute. What sense was there to be made from all these lists? You couldn't buy a program that solved murders. Hope figured she might as well just write all the information down in a little notebook, for all the good her computer was doing her.

Hope pictured herself with a notebook and a trench coat. Forget it. The notebook wouldn't do any good either. Who am I fooling? she thought. I'm no Nancy Drew. She felt a stab of despair. Despair that she couldn't do anything. Despair that she'd never see April again.

I need more facts, Hope thought gloomily. Facts. Facts. Suddenly, the cursor seemed to blink more brightly. That was the one thing a computer *could* give her. Facts. For starters, Hope had all kinds of facts about all the kids at school who'd signed up for her computer dating service. She'd gotten an impressive turnout, too. Even a lot of happy couples had filled out questionnaires—just to see who they got matched up with.

Hope cleared her computer screen and typed in the command to call up the dating program. She didn't really believe a computer could figure out your dream date—especially since she'd wound up matched with Winston Purdy III, the biggest nerd at Paradiso High. Okay, they did have a common interest in computers, and they both got excellent grades. But Winston was about as exciting as a plastic protractor.

Now, Jess . . . Hope felt his hand on hers again, and remembered the way they'd looked into each other's eyes. It hadn't been her imagination, had it? She thought about the way he'd touched her cheek when she'd gotten out of his car in town last night, the gentleness of his fingers on her face. Jess. What would it feel like to kiss him? To feel their arms around each other. . . .

Then she thought of Lacey Pinkerton pulling back from Jess's car, wearing a smug little smirk. It had been too dark to see the whole thing, but it didn't take too much imagination—

BEEP! Words appeared on her computer screen, relieving her from reliving that scene for the fiftieth time. A MATCH MADE IN PARADISO. Hope chuckled. She'd been pretty pleased with herself for coming up with that. She tapped away at the computer keys, calling up the questionnaire form she'd had all the bachelors and bachelorettes fill out.

Name. Interests. Favorite hobby. Favorite sport. Favorite color. Favorite food. Least favorite hobby, sport, etc. Ideal way to spend a date. (That one had gotten some pretty racy responses.) Most romantic place you can imagine. Biggest turn on. Biggest turn off. There were several pages of questions. Hope had even had people fill in their favorite candy, flowers, and clothing sizes, in case anyone wanted to buy a gift for his or her dream date once they'd been matched up. That part was down at the end of the questionnaire. Hat size. Shoe size.

Shoe size? "Bingo!" Hope shouted out loud. Nancy Drew, move over! She pushed her chair away from her computer and stood up. She had to call the sheriff right away to see if he had any more information on that footprint.

Before she got out the bedroom door, the phone rang. Her mother picked it up immediately. "Hello?" she heard Leanne Hubbard say from the kitchen. "Oh, hello, Sheriff Rodriguez."

Wow! ESP, thought Hope.

Leanne didn't call Hope to the phone right away, however. Hope could barely hear her speaking. "Yes . . . yes, I see . . . yes," she kept saying. Finally she said, "Thank you very much, sheriff. Hope is right here. Would you mind telling her all of this directly? It might be easier for her to hear it from you."

After a brief silence Mrs. Hubbard said, "Thank you, sheriff. Hold on just a moment. Hope? Hope, honey!"

Hope raced into the kitchen and took the receiver from her mother. "Sheriff Rodriguez? The footprint, right?" she said, her words spilling out on top of each other.

"Excuse me, Hope?" the sheriff asked.

"You're calling to tell me about the footprint. The sneaker," Hope said.

"Oh. Well, no. Not yet. We won't have the full story on that until tomorrow."

"Oh." Hope sat down at the kitchen table. Behind her, she could hear her mother making herself a slice of toast.

"But I have some other news for you," the sheriff said. Hope noticed that his voice was tight. She felt herself stiffen too. But how much worse could it get? "The autopsy report came in," the sheriff went on. "Hope, I don't want to shock you. But you're bound to hear it soon enough anyway. Willa Flicker was just in here, and I'm sure the whole town will know by mid-morning."

"What?" Hope asked tensely. "Sheriff, what is it?"

"Hope, your cousin April was killed between ten and eleven at night," Sheriff Rodriguez's voice came over the wire. "And she was pregnant."

"Oh," Hope said. So much for keeping Spike's secret. Dumb, Hope Hubbard, she told herself. D-U-M-B, dumb. She was supposed to be such a brain in school, and she hadn't even thought about how they'd find out about April when they did the autopsy.

"Hope?" Sheriff Rodriguez was saying. "Did you know about this?"

Hope bit her lip. She'd made a promise to Spike. "Sheriff . . . I'm shocked," she said. That much was actually true.

"I see," came Sheriff Rodriguez's voice. "Well,

tell me this, then. What do you know about your cousin and Jess Gardner?"

"Jess?" Hope felt herself rising to her feet.

"Yes. I got a tip that he was seen driving around with April the night of the murder."

Hope felt as if the air had suddenly gotten heavy. So Lacey and Penny weren't the only ones who'd heard that. "Well, maybe he was giving her a ride someplace," she said slowly. "They *were* friends."

"Just friends?" the sheriff probed. "Hope, I want you to be frank with me."

"Just friends," Hope said.

"Are you sure?" the sheriff pressed. "If Jess Gardner was the father of April's baby, then I'd say he's our number one suspect."

Hope's throat felt dry. "Sheriff Rodriguez, there's no way Jess could be involved in April's death. I know it."

"You do?" the sheriff said. "And how do you know that?"

Hope shrugged miserably, even though the sheriff couldn't see her. "I just do," she said.

"And what do you know about Jess and a certain girl named Michelle Wheeler?" Sheriff Rodriguez asked.

Michelle Wheeler? "Oh, yeah, well, people around school say she, um, got into trouble last year right before she moved away," Hope said. "But Jess didn't have anything to do with it. It was some older guy from out of town."

"Is that right?" Sheriff Rodriguez said. "Because Jess Gardner was seen driving around with Michelle at about that time. It seems as if there might be some kind of pattern here."

"Sheriff, Jess Gardner was not the one who got April pregnant," Hope insisted. Behind her, she heard her mother's loud gasp. Oh, no, thought Hope. Now Mom knows what they're saying about Jess, too.

"Hope," the sheriff was saying gently over the phone, "you might like Jess Gardner. But you can't rule out anyone."

"But sheriff . . ." Hope protested. "He wasn't the one!"

"Are you sure you're not basing your opinion on how you feel about Jess, Hope? He *is* a very nice-looking young man."

Hope yanked on the telephone cord in frustration and embarrassment. "Sheriff Rodriguez, I happen to know that Jess is not the father."

"You can't possibly know that," the sheriff said. Then, after a moment's pause, he added, "Unless you know who is."

Now I've done it, Hope thought. She wanted to hide under the kitchen table and never come out again.

"Hope?" Sheriff Rodriguez prompted. "You must tell me." His voice was soft, but insistent.

Hope thought of the promise she'd made to Spike. Spike, whom April loved. Spike, who loved April.

"Don't you want to find out who killed your cousin?" the sheriff asked.

Hope nodded into the telephone. "Yes, but he didn't do it either. He loved her."

"Who? Who loved her?" the sheriff asked. Hope was silent. "Hope, I can put you under oath and make you tell me," the sheriff said.

Hope knew it was pointless. Half the kids at Paradiso High knew about Spike and April. If she didn't tell the sheriff, someone else would. "Spike," she finally said into the telephone. "Spike Navarrone. He was April's boyfriend, but they didn't want her parents to know." She'd spilled it. She'd spilled Spike's secret. "But I'm sure Spike didn't kill April either. Not him or Jess," Hope said.

"Maybe not," the sheriff said. "But we have to start the investigation somewhere. Thank you."

"Sure," Hope said, but she wished she'd never gotten out of bed that morning.

"I'll call you when I find out about those footprints," the sheriff added, as if to make up for turning Hope into a traitor.

"Okay," Hope said. But she just didn't feel that

excited about the footprint anymore. "Good-bye, sheriff." She hung up the phone.

Her mother sat down at the table with her toast and a cup of black coffee and fixed Hope with her gaze. "So April was pregnant."

Hope nodded.

"I see," said Leanne. She took a sip of her coffee. "Quite a scandal for my holier-than-thou brother, Reverend Perfect."

Hope willed herself not to say anything. She'd said more than enough already, and it wasn't even eight-thirty.

Her mother seemed to soften. "Poor April," she added. Then, "Hope, honey, aren't you going to eat anything?"

Hope shook her head.

"Not even if I make you your favorite breakfast?" her mom coaxed. "Bacon and eggs and pancakes . . ."

Hope didn't have any appetite.

"Sweetie, I've never seen you skip breakfast in your whole life," Leanne Hubbard said. Her face was creased with concern.

"Mom, I'm all right," Hope assured her. But she didn't really believe her own words. How was Spike going to feel about her now that she'd given his name to Sheriff Rodriguez? Hope had his locker combination in her backpack. When she brought his things to him after school, she'd just have to explain the best she could and hope he didn't think she was a capital *R* Rat.

But something else was bothering Hope. All the sheriff's talk about Jess and April and Jess and Michelle Wheeler. And that business between Lacey and Jess in town last night. Suppose, just suppose, that Spike only thought he'd been the one to get April pregnant. Suppose, just suppose, that was one of the things April had wanted to talk to Hope about right before she'd been killed.

Hope didn't want to think it. Still, the sheriff's words rang in her head. *You can't rule out anyone.*

But Jess and Spike? They were April's friends. They cared about her. They would be as happy as Hope to see justice served. She didn't believe for a second that either one of them could be April's killer. She would bet her life on it.

Hope shivered as the thought came to her: maybe that's what she already had done.

CHAPTER 12

The dazzling morning sunshine poured through Lacey's bedroom windows, making her powder blue room bright and cheerful. It was a gorgeous Wednesday morning.

Today I'm gonna look extra foxy, she told herself.

But as she stepped into lacy pink leggings, she winced in pain as the material touched her skin. Her golden glow and high-spirited mood turned sour. One look at the backs of her legs instantly reminded her of last night's episode with Daddy, the most recent in a long history of horror. A new kind of layered look: new bruises on top of old ones. She remembered the pain pulsating throughout her body and became scared all over again.

She slumped down on a blue footrest and gently massaged the backs of her legs. As she caught sight of her frightened face in the mirror, she heard her father's words exactly: "You and your do-gooder friends are going to destroy me! My mall will die!" And she remembered every crack of his belt as it thrashed against her legs, over and over again.

I thought I was your little princess. Why do you take all your problems out on me, Daddy? she thought. It's not my fault.

My life is hopeless. What's happening to me? Every boy in this whole damn town used to offer his left arm for me. And his right arm, too! Just to be near me. To touch this perfect body. And now look at me—I can't even show it off.

Lacey ripped off her new tights and tried to tear them into shreds, hopelessly tugging the stretchy material every which way until she threw them at herself in the mirror. She watched as the wad of cloth fell limply to the ground.

Come on, Lacey, get ahold of yourself.

She grabbed another pair of tights, a brighter pink but solid, and pulled them on. She looked at herself and forced a smile.

Well, at least my face is fine, she thought. No one will ever know. No one!

Lacey thought about how April had spied through the living-room window just a few days ago, the day before she was murdered. She was the only person ever to have witnessed one of Daddy's beatings, and Lacey had wanted to kill April for finding out. She had been so humiliated and ashamed.

Daddy would have killed her if he had known, she figured. The thought flickered in her mind that maybe he *had* seen her peering in the window, but she quickly brushed it away. Daddy got out of control sometimes, but he never *meant* to hurt anyone.

April. Lacey still had a sour feeling over losing the Peach Blossom contest to April Lovewell. The same April who had once told Lacey she'd give anything just to be Lacey for a day.

I doubt it, April, Lacey thought. How'd you like to be Lacey for a day when Daddy's home waiting for you with a belt in one hand and a whiskey in the other? How'd you like to have one welt for every time you've failed? Failed to win Pretty Peggy Sue. Failed to beat Emily Gilman in the talent contest. Failed with Jess. Failed with Vaughn. Failed with Daddy. Failed with Mommy. You're better off being dead April than live Lacey!

The tears started to flow uncontrollably as Lacey crumpled to the floor in a huddled mass. She pulled her arms and legs in, curling herself into a little ball. Small. So small so that she'd disappear.

"Buenos días, señorita. Good morning, Lacey." A cheerful voice blared over the intercom. Paulita, the Pinkertons' cook, came through loud and clear.

"Don't be late for school, señorita. Manuel has brought your car up front for you. Lacey, sweetie, are you there?" she asked.

"I'm coming!" Lacey shouted from the floor.

"Oh, and Lacey," Paulita continued, "your father left early for Los Angeles. He says he loves you and will see you tonight when he gets home. He has left you a present in the front hall, señorita. And don't slam the door when you leave. Your mother is still sleeping. If you wake her up, she'll kill you. Have a nice day, señorita."

Why don't they all just leave me alone! "Leave me alone!" she screamed.

Finally, Lacey got up the energy to pick herself up and go to school. *Maybe if I get out of this horrible place I'll feel better,* she thought. The sooner the better. She hurried to grab her bag and throw on a pair of shoes and, like a bolt of lightning, she ripped opened her door and ran down the stairs.

At the foot of the staircase she stopped for a second as she saw the housekeeper—the second one hired this month—whose name she didn't even know yet, sweeping up some broken glass. It wasn't the first time Daddy had thrown his whiskey bottle against the fireplace.

The housekeeper gave her a sympathetic look,

but Lacey was far from comforted. She felt exposed.

"*Pobrecita. Dios mio,*" the housekeeper said. Poor little one.

Lacey pretended not to understand her. She rushed for the door, only to find a red rose on the side table in the front hall. Next to it was an envelope with her name on it. Lacey tore it open, not even batting an eye at the sight of a stack of crisp hundred-dollar bills with a little note clipped to it. *Love, Daddy.*

Like hell! In a rage, Lacey tore the bills in half, one by one, and threw them on the floor. She opened the door and slammed it behind her as hard as possible.

Shaking with anger, Lacey ran for the car and pulled out of the driveway in a flash, barrelling down Winding Hill Road as fast as she could, her foot pushing the gas pedal to the floor.

She felt the wind against her face. Faster, faster down the hill. If she got up enough speed, maybe she could escape her own thoughts. Wind—just wind and speed. No thoughts or feelings.

As she took a wide turn around the bend, an oncoming car swerved to avoid a collision and blasted its horn at her. Lacey honked back, driving into the furious, compressed sound.

She raced past Kiki's house. Kiki's younger brothers were outside on the front lawn, watching the pool maintenance men. They waved to Lacey, but she didn't bother to wave back.

As she rounded the next bend, she saw two familiar faces walking up the street. Kiki and Vaughn. At first she sped past them. But she couldn't resist. She slammed on the brakes and backed up, screeching to a halt in front of them.

"Hi, guys, I didn't see you at first." Lacey leaned out of the open top of the Ferrari. "Great outfit, Kiki." She chuckled at Kiki, who was dressed in an ultra-conservative navy blue blazer and matching skirt, a white button-down shirt, and dark tie. Her blue and white polka-dotted sneakers gave the outfit its only flair. She had a green and black SCAM button pinned on her lapel and carried a beat-up brown clipboard with well-thumbed petitions attached.

Kiki took the compliment with a large grain of salt. "Thanks, Lacey," she said with a forced smile, determined not to let Lacey get to her. "Raven suggested I wear it. It's my canvassing outfit."

Lacey sneered. "That figures. Well, with Raven choosing your wardrobe, I'm sure you'll get *lots* of signatures."

Lacey watched with glee as Kiki's mouth tightened and her eyes narrowed.

"Don't listen to her, Kiki," Vaughn said, putting

a calming hand on Kiki's shoulder. He turned to Lacey. "Gee, Lacey. I can see you're your usual sweet self today. What happened? Your dad knock a few zeroes off your allowance?"

"No, it's just that some ex-friends of mine decided to ruin my father's life, that's all." Lacey shook her head. "Look at you two. Raven's goody-goods. What's the matter? You guys don't want to have a mall like the rest of America? Is Raven teaching you how wonderful it is to be deprived? Or is she history already? I mean you two are up together awfully early. . . ."

"Bug off, Lacey. I'm warning you." Vaughn said.

But she continued. "Sure gave her up fast enough. Was it the poor life that got to you, or did you just think it was wrong to have an affair with your boss? You know, you and Kiki are perfect for each other anyway. You're both so dull." She glared at Kiki. "Did you stay in some cheap hotel last night or did the Cutters let you spend the night, like I used to?"

"Shut up, Lacey!" Vaughn was furious. "You don't know what you're talking about. Kiki and I are friends. That's all. You ever hear of just being friends?"

"Yeah. Like we all used to be. Remember, Lacey? We were best friends," Kiki said.

"What do you know about being friends?" Lacey

136

asked accusingly. "You wouldn't even withdraw from the Peach Blossom contest for me. Like a true friend would have done."

"You tried to bribe me to quit," she said. "That's not friendship!"

"Give me a break, Kiki. Don't give me that moral rap. You're as heartless as anyone I know. Your friendship is like a snakebite." Lacey paused, then reminded Kiki, "Look at April. You were her friend, too."

"Huh? What is that supposed to mean?" Kiki was confused.

"Don't you think I remember what you said to her the day before she was murdered? 'I'm going to strangle you.' Those were your words exactly. Isn't it interesting that that's how she was killed?" Lacey insinuated.

Vaughn stepped in between the two girls. His face was dark and hard. "If you don't cool it, Lacey, I'll be the one to do some strangling. Leave her alone." He clenched and unclenched his fists by his sides.

"Gee, you're so tough, Vaughn. Always solving problems with your fists," Lacey said. She felt her heart quicken with a too-familiar anxiety as Vaughn's right hand rose above his shoulder, open, threatening. Who did he think he was? "Come on!

Hit me. Go ahead, Vaughn. Hit me. I can take the pain. Come on!"

"Vaughn, no!" Kiki cried. Vaughn looked confused, then startled to see how far he'd gone. His hand dropped, and Kiki went on: "I don't believe you, Lacey. You're really insane. I made that comment about an art project. You think I'd kill April because she could paint better than me? That's like me thinking you killed April because she won Peach Blossom Queen. Just like the article said."

"Maybe I did!" Lacey shouted at the top of her lungs.

"Hey, will you all shut up!" came an angry voice from an open window. "Shut up or I'll call the cops!"

There followed a long silence. It wasn't even eight o'clock in the morning, and Lacey had burned up enough steam for the entire day. She looked at the embarrassed faces of Vaughn and Kiki. For a moment she wanted to apologize and make amends. But she just couldn't.

"Look, Lacey," Kiki pleaded. "Why don't you just cool out? We've all been so upset over April's murder. No one is themselves these days. I think Winston Purdy was right when he said we should all stay together. What do you say? What happened to my loyal friend?"

"Sorry, Kiki, but your loyal friend is the *only* one

138

who really is loyal," Lacey said, pointing a finger at herself. "That's right, me! Look at you guys wearing Raven's tacky buttons. Who's kidding who? Kiki, you know your father will make a fortune if they build the new mall. And Vaughn, remember who your father is? I'm surprised he even lets you into the house. You'd better trade in the Jaguar for a ten-speed. Sorry, guys, but I don't see the loyalty."

"Speaking of loyalty, Lacey . . ." Vaughn said. "You wouldn't even be driving that car if it wasn't for me. How soon we forget. 'Daddy will kill me if he finds out.' Isn't that what you told me, Lacey? 'Please, oh, please, help me, Vaughn. I'll do anything.' Remember, Lacey?"

"That was a secret just between us." She gave Vaughn a cold, hard stare. "See, you really can't keep your word, either. Like I said, you and Kiki are perfect for each other. Don't bother inviting me to the wedding. I'm busy that day." She turned to Kiki and pointed a warning finger at her. "And you'd better not ask Vaughn what we're talking about. It's none of your damn business!"

CHAPTER 13

Kiki watched Lacey take off with a squeal of tires and the smell of burning rubber. The Ferrari hurtled down Winding Hill Road, coming awfully close to the edge as it swerved around a sharp curve.

"Big Foot, pressing down heavy on the accelerator," Kiki commented. It was a mean thing to say, and Kiki wished she hadn't. Lacey was super sensitive about her large feet. But that remark about strangling April was a low blow, even for Lacey.

"Aaargh!" Vaughn growled as the Ferrari roared out of sight. He was lunging first in one direction, then another, until he finally planted his loafer violently against the side of a huge old sycamore tree. "I must have been blind!" he shouted.

"Vaughn, calm down," Kiki said. She'd never seen him like this. "What do you mean?"

"To go out with Lacey Pinkerton. I must have been blinded by the way she looks."

Kiki sighed. "She can be pretty fun to hang out with, too. And she treats you well when you're on her good side."

"Yeah." Vaughn's anger had passed like a summer storm. "Lacey knows how to have a good time. That's for sure. Then the spell wears off, and you get a look at her riding around on her broomstick."

Kiki shrugged, balancing the Stop the Mall petition on her arm. "Yeah, I guess that's true." Still, as the sound of the Ferrari dissolved in the tranquil morning, Kiki felt a pang. She missed Lacey. The Lacey who came over after school and hung out by Kiki's pool. The Lacey who brought the latest CDs over and blasted them on Kiki's stereo as they both danced around her room. The Lacey who had arranged for the use of the Pinkertons' private jet to take them on a shopping spree in Beverly Hills.

Kiki didn't feel quite so down on Lacey as Vaughn did, even though she knew Lacey deserved it. "I don't know. I mean, I'm really mad at her. But at the same time, I sort of miss going over to Rosa's with her for our usual morning iced tea," Kiki said, more to herself than to Vaughn. What made it even worse was knowing that there was no going back. Sure, she could probably make up with Lacey, but could she close her eyes to Lacey's true

141

colors? Could she go back to being the wimp she'd once been, willing to let Lacey take the lead? Never!

"Keeks," Vaughn said, "forget that girl. She doesn't deserve your friendship. You wanna go to Rosa's? You and I can go over there. Let's go down to my house and get the Jag. We've got some time before school, and we got a lot of signatures."

Kiki glanced down at the pages of names on the petition. "Yeah, we did great, didn't we?"

Vaughn grinned. "We sure did. I'm sure Raven will want to see this."

"Raven. Yeah, of course." Kiki laughed. "We both know the real reason you want to go to Rosa's so badly this morning."

"This morning and every morning," Vaughn admitted. "I really like her."

"Raven's wonderful," Kiki agreed.

"Wonderful, beautiful, clever . . . What are we waiting for?" Vaughn was blushing as if Raven were his first girlfriend. Which she wasn't. Tall, muscular, and handsome, Vaughn had half the female population of Paradiso High driving back and forth in front of the Cutters' stone mansion.

Kiki and Vaughn headed down Winding Hill Road to his house. "So, Kiki, speaking of romance," he said, "I haven't seen you with Bobby lately."

Kiki felt a tremor of guilt. "Yeah, well . . . with

everything that's happened, I guess I just needed some time to myself." She knew Bobby felt bad. The night before, he'd asked her point blank on the phone if she wanted to break up. He'd sounded so hurt. And he cared for her so much. "We'll go to the movies this weekend," she'd promised.

Kiki followed Vaughn through the gate in the stone wall around the Cutter estate. Bobby was smart and caring and decent. So how come she didn't feel better when she was thinking about him?

Vaughn led the way down a brick path. With its stately elm and oak trees, its ivy-covered stone walls and twisty walkways, the Cutters' place was more transplanted New England than sprawling, green California. "Bobby's a good guy," Vaughn said. "But you've gotta do what feels right to you."

"I guess." Kiki shrugged. She had know Vaughn all her life. When they had been growing up, he and Lars, Jr., were like her brothers. She and Vaughn had always gone to each other for romantic advice. But right now, Kiki didn't feel like talking about Bobby. The problem was, she didn't really know how she felt. She changed the subject.

"So are you and your father still on speaking terms?" More than a few people this morning had been surprised to see Vaughn Cutter out petitioning against his father's pet project.

Vaughn rolled his eyes. "Don't you notice that we're going straight to the garage? Do not stop back at the house, do not see Mom and Dad, do not pass go, do not collect two hundred dollars." Vaughn took his car keys out of his jeans pocket and unlocked the garage. The beat-up maroon Jaguar was parked next to Mr. Cutter's Mercedes and Mrs. Cutter's Lincoln.

Kiki climbed into the passenger seat of the Jag. "Didn't it help that you decided to go to Dartmouth in September?" she asked, buckling her seat belt.

Vaughn started the engine. "Nah. That's just what I'm supposed to do. I mean, in Dad's mind there was never even any question. He went there, Junior, the perfect son, is there, and I'll be there too. But going against Dad on the mall, well, that's not in the plan. He won't even listen to my side. He's furious. He's acting like I killed someone." Vaughn shook his head. "Oops. Wrong expression. Man, you manage to forget about it for a second, but it keeps coming back to haunt you."

Vaughn pulled out of the garage, closing it behind him with the remote he had in the car. "I can't understand why it's taking them so long to catch the guy who did it," he added tightly.

"Vaughn, it's only been a few days," Kiki said. But she knew how he felt. Paradiso wouldn't begin to heal until April's killer was found. "What do you think about that rumor about Jess?"

A dark scowl stole across Vaughn's face. "When I catch the person who started it—" Vaughn slammed his hand against the steering wheel. Hard.

Kiki gave a start. Vaughn wasn't kidding. Not too many people knew it, but under the laid-back attitude, Vaughn had a real temper. And Jess Gardner was his best friend.

"Besides, what if Jess *was* riding around with April?" Vaughn went on angrily. "That doesn't mean a thing," he said, pounding the dashboard for emphasis, until on the last blow, a jagged crack appeared on the glass covering the instrument panel.

"Hey, mellow," Kiki said. "It's just gossip. Ignore it." Vaughn's outbursts were beginning to scare her. She noticed that the Jag's clock was smashed, and its steering wheel was pocked with tiny dents. Was it all part of the car's generally dilapidated condition, or was this a side of Vaughn Cutter Kiki hadn't known before?

"I'm sorry," Vaughn said. "It's just . . . I don't know how to deal with it sometimes. I get so mad, it feels like it's gotta go somewhere."

"I know," Kiki said, laying a hand on his forearm. "And there sure is a lot to be mad about lately, isn't there?"

As they got out on the road, Vaughn began to

relax. Maybe he just needed to get off the Hill. Away from his father's house. Away from Lacey's. Away from the subject of April's murder. Kiki tried to stick with safe conversation—like how many people had signed the mall petition, and how much fun it was to catch a ride in the Jag, and how she hoped Oberlin College would call and tell her she'd been accepted off the waiting list.

Maybe it was working. Or maybe it was Raven. As they got closer to Rosa's, Vaughn began to grin again. Kiki gave an inward sigh of relief. He sped the last few miles and peeled into the café's little parking lot. He practically flew from the car through the front door of the café, leaving Kiki to trail after him.

Raven wasn't too upset to see Vaughn, either. She stopped right in the middle of the café, a plate of *huevos rancheros* in either hand, and turned her face up to Vaughn's for a loud smack on the lips.

"Raven, the customers," Mr. Cruz said in a thick Mexican accent from behind the counter.

"Okay, Papa," Raven said. She winked at Vaughn and delivered the two plates of eggs to a table where Willa Flicker, the editor of the *Record*, sat with another woman Kiki didn't recognize.

"Hi, Mr. Cruz," Vaughn said.

"Hello, Vaughn," Mr. Cruz said. With his

146

accent, it sounded sort of like "A-low Bone."
"Hello, Miss De Santis."

Kiki smiled. She and Vaughn took seats at the counter. Raven came back over, wiped her hands on her apron, and sat down with them. "How'd it go?" she asked eagerly. "Oh, listen, can I get you guys anything?"

"I'll have some coffee," Vaughn said. "And it went really well. We got three pages of signatures. It was great. Except that it got spoiled at the end by a guest appearance from our very own cheerleader for Daddy's Mall."

"Lacey?" Raven said. She got up, took a cup and saucer from under the counter, and put them in front of Vaughn. "Anything for you, Kiki?"

"Well, speaking of Lacey," Kiki said a little sheepishly, "I guess I'll have a glass of iced tea."

Raven got the coffeepot and poured Vaughn a cup of coffee. "One iced tea, coming right up," she said. Kiki watched her scoop ice into a tall glass and fill it with strong, dark tea from a large metal urn near the coffee machine. She came back to the counter and set it down at Kiki's place. "Now, what were we talking about? Oh, Lacey. Yeah." Kiki noticed a funny look on Raven's face. She couldn't quite read it. "I wonder," Raven said slowly, "what it would be like to have to live with her parents."

"Cal the man and Darling Darla?" Vaughn said. "Hell, I'm sure. About like living with my dad."

"Raven!" Mr. Cruz sounded less good humored than he had before. "Your order's up." A plate of pancakes steamed on the shelf window between the kitchen and the counter area.

" 'Scuse me for a sec," Raven said. She went over to the window and grabbed the plate. Vaughn's eyes followed her all the way across the café and back.

"Why were you thinking about Mr. and Mrs. Pinkerton?" Vaughn asked when she returned.

There was that unreadable look again. A little furrowing of the eyebrows. "Oh, um, I don't know," Raven said.

"They're pretty horrible," Kiki confirmed. "Even though they give Lacey everything she wants." She sighed. "But Lacey, well, maybe you guys don't believe it, but she is not all bad."

"You mean she's got more than *two* faces?" Raven joked, her dark eyes flashing.

Kiki laughed too. "But I really mean it," she said. "I don't think it's fair to judge Lacey right now. Her or anybody. I mean, no one's at their best these days. . . ."

"Well, maybe when they reschedule the Peach Blossom Festival, it'll give people something else to think about," Raven said.

Kiki felt uncomfortable. "I don't know, Raven. I still think it's a bad idea. Look, there's a killer out there somewhere. How can we go around electing queens and having balls and festivals?" She hadn't meant to bring up April's murder again, but it was unavoidable. It was too tough to forget it for very long.

"But Kiki," Raven said, "if we stop going on with our lives, the murderer—whoever he is—will have made all of us his victims."

Kiki took a long, cold sip of her iced tea. "Maybe you're right. But it's so hard to go on with everything when you're looking over your shoulder every five minutes thinking half the people you know are going around with blunt instruments." She gave a short, tense laugh. "You know, yesterday I even started to think that maybe Mr. Wool—"

"Raven!" Mr. Cruz's voice interrupted her from the other end of the counter. "Table two. They want their check."

Raven was up again. This time when she came back, she didn't sit down. "Mama's sick," she said. "And it's pretty busy this morning. Kiki, what were you saying?"

"Mr. Woolery," Kiki said. "I guess I was feeling so scared about the murder that for a few minutes yesterday I even started thinking that maybe he could have done it."

149

"Dreamboat?" Vaughn said. "No way. He's a sensitive artist. Besides, why would he have any reason to kill April?"

Kiki shrugged. "I don't know, but I went into the art room, and he had all her work laid out around him on the floor, and he had this weird look on his face. I got the creeps. Pretty dumb, huh?"

"I guess anything's possible," Vaughn said. "But I wouldn't put my money on Woolery."

Kiki finished her iced tea and banged the glass down on the counter. "I suppose not," she said. She wished she felt more convinced.

CHAPTER 14

If I were my computer, all odds would point to Spike, Hope thought, staring at the crinkled piece of paper in her hand. She had arrived at school early so that no one would see her at Spike's locker, and packed his books, dirt-caked gym shoes, and T-shirt stained with motorcycle grease in her backpack. As she started closing the locker, she had noticed the crumpled-up note in the back. She took it out and smoothed it open.

Meet me at the usual place after dinner tonight, it read. It wasn't signed, but Hope knew her cousin's handwriting.

The door to Spike's locker still wide open, Hope read and reread the note. What if April had written it the day she'd been killed? That would mean she'd planned to meet Spike the night of the murder—that Spike might have been the last person to

151

see her. Spike, not Jess. What if Spike really had—
No! No way. Maybe my computer would say yes,
Hope thought. But my heart says no. It wasn't
Spike.

She'd just have to give him the note with the rest
of his stuff and see what he said. She had a vision of
Spike as he had been the other day, sleepless and
unshaven, waving around that wrench. A wrench!
Suddenly Hope felt cold. What if, just suppose, just
pretend, there was the teensiest fraction of a
chance that Spike was the killer. And she was heading out there, to his lonely, remote trailer, all by
herself.

She had the urge to throw all his things back in
his locker and let him come pick them up himself.
But she talked herself out of it. She trusted Spike.
And he'd asked her to do him a favor. Besides,
Hope had already been out to Spike's once, and
she'd been perfectly safe. Why would he wait until
her second visit out there? No, Spike was no killer.
He was just sad and angry. Like she was. And if she
didn't go out to his place and explain what had
happened with Sheriff Rodriguez, Spike would
think she had broken her promise to him.

Hope caught a movement out of the corner of
her eye. All of a sudden, she realized she wasn't
alone. Coming down the hall were Lacey, Renée,
and Penny. Oh, no! The Pinks. Hope slammed

Spike's locker shut and stuffed the note from April into the back pocket of her jeans. There would be more than enough rumors going around school today once the news from the autopsy report got out. Hope didn't want to start any more. She raced away before they had a chance to ask any questions. She didn't hear anyone behind her, but just to make sure, she took a sharp right around the corridor that led to Principal Appleby's office.

And she stopped stock still. Ahead of her were two familiar figures. She knew them even from the back—Uncle Ward, his full head of graying hair cropped close, and Aunt Sara, with sensible shoes and her strawberry hair pulled into a severe bun at the nape of her neck. Hope's first reaction was to turn around and run away.

Her second reaction was more complicated. In Aunt Sara's strawberry bun, Hope saw April's flaming, flowing red hair. In Uncle Ward's long-legged stride, she saw April's walk. She swallowed hard, feeling the way she had at the cemetery—that she would like to close the canyon between her and the Lovewells, to make peace and console them and be consoled herself.

But Hope knew it was useless. Her uncle only *talked* peace. When it came to action, he made accusations about her to the sheriff. She stood and watched April's parents turn in to the principal's office. She couldn't approach them.

But she could follow them. Their visit had to be connected to April's death. If Hope wanted to gather clues, she needed to know what Uncle Ward and Aunt Sara had to say to Principal Appleby.

She approached his office, stopping just short of the partially opened door. It led to the outer room, where Ms. Nyhart, Principal Appleby's secretary, sat. Peeking in, Hope could see that the principal's door was shut. But her uncle's voice was loud and angry. She had no trouble hearing him out in the hall.

"Sorry?" he was yelling, his voice trembling with anger. "Sorry, Mr. Appleby? Sorry hardly seems to be enough when you are responsible for what happened to my daughter!"

Principal Appleby? Responsible for killing April? Dwight the Dweeb a cold-blooded killer? Impossible.

Hope had to strain to hear his answer. "Excuse me?" he squeaked. "Responsible? Um, she was a student in my school, yes, but I don't see how—"

"How that makes you to blame for my daughter being taken from this earth, brutally and before her time?" Ward Lovewell growled. Aunt Sara let out a sob. "Well, let's see, Mr. Appleby. *Principal* Appleby," Uncle Ward corrected himself. "You do

154

agree that you are responsible for your teachers at this school? Or do you have no control over your own staff?"

He has no control over his own staff, Hope thought. At that moment, she felt a huge burst of sympathy for Dwight the Dweeb. She pressed toward the door for his response. "Um, ah, yes, of course I do—I am. Yes, yes."

"You hire the best teachers for our children?" Uncle Ward pressed on.

"Yes. Naturally," Principal Appleby said. A little note of pride even slipped into his voice.

"And you make sure they understand the relationship between teacher and student?" Aunt Sara put in.

Hope imagined Principal Appleby bobbing his head up and down in a hyperactive nod.

"Then do you think you can tell me why one of your teachers took our little girl to a deserted wasteland, well outside of school hours?" Reverend Lovewell thundered. His voice was loud enough to be heard by several students halfway down the hall. They froze, riveted.

"A teacher at Paradiso High? Who? Where? When?" Mr. Appleby asked, in a kind of nervous pant.

"You don't know who? You say you're responsible for the people you hire, yet you don't know that your art teacher took our dear April, may she rest in peace, to a very secluded and very dangerous place?" Uncle Ward yelled.

"Mr. Woolery?" Shock rang in Principal Appleby's voice. "Where?"

Uncle Ward kept lashing Mr. Woolery with his words. "Yes, Mr. Woolery. He took April to the scrublands!"

Hope felt a swelling wave of anger and disgust. Of course he had. He had taken her sketching there, because he believed in her talent as an artist. He had put in his own time to help her. He was no murderer. He was April's favorite teacher. He was a friend.

"He took her there," Uncle Ward went on, "and —and, well, Mr. Appleby, our little girl was in the family way when she was taken from us!"

Hope stifled a groan. If the word hadn't leaked out yet, it was about to start. The group of kids down the hall exchanged startled looks.

"In the—family way?" Principal Appleby echoed. "And you believe Mark Woolery was responsible?"

Aunt Sara answered this time, her voice full of indignation and pain. "Mr. Appleby, why else would that man take my daughter to a deserted place at sunrise?"

"To draw it?" Principal Appleby was an A-1

dweeb, but for once Hope applauded his words. "Reverend Lovewell, I was informed about that trip, and I was also informed that it took place with your, er, blessing."

"We were innocently misled about this man's character," Ward Lovewell said. "And a man who is capable of doing that to a—a child, well, he could be capable of murder, too."

Principal Appleby seemed to be knocked speechless. The tension-filled pause was broken by the sound of his office door opening. "Good day," Uncle Ward said forbiddingly. "You shall hear from my lawyer!"

Hope spun on her heel and took off down the hall so that she wouldn't get caught. She rushed past the open-mouthed cluster of kids who had been listening too and turned the corner. From there, she peeked back around to watch her aunt and uncle coming out of the office. Rage and pain tightened every muscle in their faces.

Hope was torn by anger and sorrow. How could you expect them not to look that way? April had been senselessly murdered. Their only child. Their lives would never be full again. But how could it help to turn their grief on everybody around them? Hope watched them march down the hall and toward the front entrance to the school. Their backs were rigid, and their bitterness enveloped them like a noxious cloud.

First they had accused Hope. Now they were accusing Mr. Woolery. Who would be the next victim of their broken hearts?

CHAPTER 15

Bored to death. Lacey sat in Schwob's chemistry class, counting the minutes. It wasn't the first time, and it certainly wouldn't be the last. With so much going on, she was having a lot of trouble even pretending to pay attention to his babbling. News about April continued to surface, and Lacey couldn't sit still.

Twenty-five minutes until lunch. This class will never end. It's so boring! she thought. Lacey looked around the classroom. On her left, Winston Purdy III sat in between her and Renée. Eddie Hagenspitzel separated her from Penny on her right. The three girls used to sit together, but Mr. Schwob had separated them for obvious reasons.

Fine, Lacey thought. But that doesn't mean we can't chat. Now that there was a murderer on the loose, you just didn't know who'd be around tomorrow to gossip with.

She took out her pad of pink notepaper and a pink fountain pen and began writing. Winston passed the notes quickly and nervously. Eddie needed a swift kick under the table to make sure he didn't open them.

"Just pass 'em along, Hagenspitzel," Lacey ordered.

Who's the father of April's baby?
Was it Spike? I say, maybe.

Lacey

Lacey, you're a poet and I didn't know it. He's obviously her killer, too. Why else would he be absent all week? He probably killed her because she wouldn't get an abortion.

Renée

Don't be so sure. Spike is *maybe* the father. Let's not forget we're dealing with April LOVEwell. April's rep. as loosest girl in town had to start somewhere. There's lots of possibilities. Woolery, for example. What do we know about him? That stuff about his downtown New York art scene past may be bull. He could be some lunatic from Bellevue.

Lacey

160

I heard Woolery taught April more than art.

Renée

I doubt it's Woolery. I'd watch out for Jess.
(Seriously, Lace.) Sweet and innocent on the
outside, but guilty as sin. Rope + wrench
+ April's *final* ride = JESS GARDNER.

Penny

Lay off, Pen. You think he'd show up for
school? He'd be in Mexico! You should have
seen his smile when I saw him at his locker.
Must have been thinking about heartthrob
Hope Hubbard. Barf! I'm in total shock.
HOPE! She's the killer! Sweet, innocent,
quiet, and honest . . . a real murderer, like
in the movies. What was she doing at Spike's
locker anyway? She was up to *something* fishy.

So who dunnit? Here's my complete list:

Spike—obvious reasons. But I doubt it. Too
cool to kill April. She wouldn't be worth
spending his life in jail over.

Woolery—he might be gorgeous, but that
never stopped anyone.

Bubba Dole—he'd kill anyone just for fun.

Winston Purdy III—only kidding.

Hope—she's gonna goof up somewhere and
get caught red-handed.

Willa Flicker—getting famous over April's murder. She'd do anything for her career.

Eddie Hagenspitzel—sickest joke of the year.

Kiki—she wanted that crown more than you'd think.

Bobby Deeter—did it for Kiki because he'd do anything for her. Just for a kiss.

Me—because she was gonna get a better grade in this stupid chemistry class.

Renée—she wore the same dress to school last week.

Penny—April is your least favorite month of the year. I didn't know you hated it *that* much.

Who did I forget?

Lacey

JESS GARDNER. (Sorry, Lacey. Face facts: they all point to Jess.)

Penny

JESS GARDNER. Sorry, Lacey. You better be careful.

Renée

CHAPTER 16

ENTER PASSWORD flashed in blue letters on the gray computer screen. The cursor blinked away, challenging Hope to discover the secret word.

WOOLERY, she typed. The sound of her fingers striking the keys echoed in the school computer room, always deserted at noon. "Shhh," she said, feeling a little silly for talking to a computer. But she didn't want anyone to catch her looking into Mr. Appleby's private files. Or trying to. The computer gave a beep. ERROR: UNACCEPTABLE CODE.

Hope sighed. MARK WOOLERY, she typed. Beep. The message repeated itself. TEACHERS. No, that wasn't the password either. Hope clicked away without success.

At least the walls of the little cubicle she sat in shielded her from view. They couldn't keep out her guilty conscience, however. This wasn't all that different from trying to pick the lock on Mr. Appleby's file drawer. Besides, if Mr. Woolery was guilty of anything, it was probably just being too good a teacher. He cared about his students. He'd recognized April's talent as an artist, and he'd done his best to encourage her.

Still, a good detective had to follow every lead, which meant that Hope needed more information on Paradiso High's resident artist and number one teacher-heartbreaker. EMPLOYEES, Hope punched into the computer. She watched the bottom of her screen for the error message.

Instead, a new message came up. LAST NAME, FIRST NAME. Hope gave a silent cheer. WOOLERY, MARK, she typed, with a feeling of satisfaction.

WOOLERY, MARK, echoed the electronic address card that appeared on her computer screen. ART. 120 WEST ORCHARD BOULEVARD. SAN PEDRO, CA 932-8762.

Hope hit the return key to call up the next document in Mr. Woolery's file.

BOARD OF EDUCATION OF THE STATE OF CALIFORNIA. APPLICATION FOR TEMPORARY PER DIEM CERTIFICATE. Per diem. Per day, Hope translated, from eleventh-grade elective Latin. Daily. Temporary daily certificate. Hmmm. That meant that Mr. Woolery didn't have his teaching license. He was temporary, on trial. Hope felt worse than ever for him. Uncle Ward and Aunt Sara's accusations were certainly not going to help secure Mr. Woolery's position at Paradiso High.

ADDRESS. SOCIAL SECURITY NUMBER. DATE OF BIRTH. Wow. Mr. Woolery wasn't that much older than some of the kids Hope would be at college with this fall. EDUCATIONAL PREPARATION. LIST ALL SCHOOLS ATTENDED, BEGINNING WITH MOST RECENT SCHOOL.

ART STUDENTS' LEAGUE, NEW YORK CITY, Mr. Woolery had filled in, following it with a list of the other schools he'd gone to. Hope pictured an only slightly younger Mr. Woolery painting away in an old but light-filled room with a view of the Empire State Building.

EMPLOYMENT HISTORY. That was short. Mr. Woolery had been a teaching assistant during college and a housepainter in New York City after he'd graduated, but Paradiso High was his first fulltime job.

PERSONAL INFORMATION. EYE COLOR: BROWN. HAIR COLOR: BROWN. HEIGHT: 6'2. WEIGHT: 195. Hope shook her head. The description definitely did not do justice to Mr. Woolery's looks. It should have said large, chocolate brown eyes with long dark lashes, thick wavy hair, great bod . . .

DISTINGUISHING MARKS: BIRTHMARK ON INSIDE OF RIGHT THIGH. Boy, some of the girls at school would give a lot for that information, Hope thought with a giggle. She heard her own laughter in the empty room, and she was instantly quiet.

ARE YOU A U.S. CITIZEN? YES. DO YOU REQUIRE SPECIAL ARRANGEMENTS BECAUSE OF A HANDICAP? NO. HAVE YOU EVER BEEN DISCHARGED FROM ANY POSITION (OTHER THAN LAYOFF DUE TO REDUCTION IN WORK FORCE)? NO. HAVE YOU EVER BEEN CONVICTED OF A LEGAL OFFENSE (OTHER THAN A TRAFFIC INFRACTION)? YES.

Yes? Mr. Woolery had been arrested? And convicted? Of what? SEE UNDER SEPARATE COVER.

Hope scrolled through the rest of Mr. Woolery's job application. There was no extra information at the end of the document. Quickly she skimmed the other documents in Mr. Woolery's file. CURRICULUM PLAN, HIGH SCHOOL ART, said one of them. STUDENT ROSTERS. That one had lists of all the students in each of Mr. Woolery's classes and their grades for the first three marking periods. Hope remembered how Eddie Hagenspitzel had tried to talk her into tampering with his grades last year. FOURTH-QUARTER SCHEDULE AND ROOM NUMBERS was the next document.

Hope went through the rest of the file, but there was no additional document on Mr. Woolery's arrest. She positioned her hands on the keyboard. MORE, she typed. She stifled a groan as the error message appeared on the bottom of the screen, accompanied by a beep. SEPARATE COVER. Beep. No. POLICE RECORDS, she tried. No. ARRESTS. CONVICTIONS. Error. Error. SECRET FILES, she typed, sure it wasn't going to get her anywhere. CRIMES, she plugged in, in desperation. JAIL.

Right. Sure, Mr. Appleby was going to have a special file called JAIL for the teachers at his school. Hope took her hands off the keys and leaned back in her chair. Mr. Woolery, a criminal! Suddenly that awful picture appeared in Hope's mind—the picture of April's stiff, cold arm. Hope felt queasy.

Beep! Hope almost tipped over in her chair as letters started appearing on her screen without her so much as hitting a key. She leaned forward in her seat. INTERTERMINAL COMMUNICATION, said the words on the monitor. Someone was sending her a message! The message began coming up on the next line. HOPE HUBBARD, it said. Suddenly Hope was aware of the tapping of keys from a cubicle on the other side of the room.

She wasn't alone! She felt her breath catch in her throat. Who was there? How did that person know what she was doing? She pushed back her chair and began to stand up so that she could look beyond the walls of the cubicle.

DON'T TRY TO FIND OUT WHO I AM flashed the next line on Hope's screen.

She sank back into her seat. Fear fluttered inside her as she waited for the rest of the message.

STOP SNOOPING. The sound of the keys being pressed rose up from a cubicle near the door to the computer room. OR YOU'RE NEXT. Hope gave a strangled cry. April's killer was in the room! She had to get out of there. She had to escape. But whoever was sending the message was right by the door. The only door. Hope was trapped!

Her breath came fast and shallow. Fear pounded in her ears. She waited for the hand around her neck. Instead, she heard the door to the computer room slam. Was she locked in? Locked in with a killer?

The seconds passed, marked by the blinking cursor on Hope's screen. The seconds turned to minutes. No more words appeared on her computer.

"Hello?" Hope called, her voice quaking. There was no response. Please, please be gone, she prayed. Please. She waited a long time, just to be sure. Was the cursor beating the final moments of her life?

She pushed back her chair, the legs making a squeaking sound against the floor. She kept her eye on the computer screen. No message came up to tell her to stay still. She stood up. Her head was visible above the walls of her cubicle. She held her breath. Nothing. No more warnings. No sounds. She took a step. Then another. Then she raced for the door. She pulled it open and burst out into the hall.

She stood panting, as if she'd just run a mile. You're fine, she told herself. You're alive. She took in huge gulps of air until she felt her pulse slowing down. Out of the corner of her eye she saw a flash of blue as someone disappeared down the next corridor. The killer! Hope looked up and down the hall again, but the person who had sent the message had disappeared.

Only now did Hope dare to sneak a look back into the computer room. Through the little window in the door, she could see that the computer screen closest to her was glowing, the power still on. Hope let herself back in and went over. The terrifying threat jumped out at her again. OR YOU'RE NEXT. She reached behind the terminal and turned the monitor off. The screen went comfortingly blank.

Hope left the room again in a hurry. Her heart was still beating double time. Somewhere in the building someone was afraid of what Hope might find out. Someone guilty. Someone who might not hesitate to kill. Again.

CHAPTER 17

"Hey, heartthrob," Raven said as Vaughn approached the tree she was sitting under. "Where've you been?" He was wearing a light blue polo shirt that made his eyes look extra blue and a pair of well-worn jeans with a rip over one of his muscular thighs.

Vaughn dropped the gym bag that he carried all his school stuff in and sat down next to her. He leaned over and kissed her on the cheek, letting his lips linger.

Raven turned toward him, feeling the way his lips brushed her face until their mouths met. She melted into their kiss, which was first soft and then more insistent. "I missed you," she said in his ear.

"What a welcome," Vaughn said huskily. "Maybe I should disappear on you more often."

"Don't you dare," Raven said. "I've been sitting

here alone eating my lunch, and you're not even going to tell me where you've been hiding?"

"All alone? I'll bet half the guys at school have come by and suddenly gotten fascinated with stopping the Greenway Mall."

"Vaughn . . . I thought we were going to hang out together!"

"Okay, okay." He laughed. "I had to go pick up Junior at the airport."

"Junior, your brother?" Raven asked. She kissed him softly on the forehead. Then on his eyelids. "If you ask me, it's kind of silly for a nineteen-year-old boy to be called Junior. What's he doing home, anyway?" She planted another kiss right on his mouth. "Isn't he supposed to be at Dartmouth?"

"Dad flew him home for a few days for some stockholders' meeting at the bank," Vaughn explained, running his hand up and down her back. "Grooming him for the family business, you know. Which should tell you that he's perfectly named. Junior—short for Dad, Junior, which is exactly what the guy is." Vaughn let his hand drop to his side. "I can't believe I'm going to have to spend my college years with him right down the hall or across campus or something."

"Hey," Raven said, trying to snuggle back into Vaughn's hug. "I'm sorry I brought him up. Now can we go back to where we were?"

171

Vaughn took Raven in his arms and gave her a long kiss. But then he pulled back again. Raven noticed the serious look in his eyes. Her forehead furrowed. "What's wrong?"

"Raven, there's something I have to show you," Vaughn said. "You're not going to like it."

Raven felt herself tense. "April," she said. "It has something to do with April, doesn't it?" The stories about April had been racing through school like a brush fire this morning.

Vaughn reached across her and grabbed his gym bag. "No."

He unzipped the bag. "When I helped Junior inside with his stuff, I saw this on the dining-room table. There were about a dozen copies, so I helped myself to one." He pulled out a sheet of paper and handed it to Raven.

DON'T LET YOUR CHILD BE NEXT! it read in bold type across the top.

"I thought you said it wasn't about April." Raven was confused.

"It isn't really," Vaughn said. "It's really about just how low my dad and Cal Pinkerton are willing to stoop to make a buck. They've taken out a full-page ad opposite Willa Flicker's editorial in the next issue of the *Record*."

We are all in a profound state of grief and shock over the loss of one of the children of our

172

community, the ad said in smaller print, beneath the headline. *As responsible citizens, we have to ask ourselves if it would have happened if our children had a safe place to meet.*

Raven felt her blood boiling. Of all the slippery, sleazy moves! "They're using April's death to try to push the mall through!"

"I told you that you wouldn't like it," Vaughn said.

Raven read the rest of the ad. It went on about the safe, clean shops and restaurants Cal Pinkerton and Lars Cutter wanted to build and the well-lit public areas within the indoor mall. Somehow they managed to make it seem as if they had designed the entire project in response to the tragedy of April's murder. *The Greenway Mall,* the advertisement concluded. *Because Paradiso will miss April Lovewell.*

"They make it sound like if there'd been a mall, April would still be around," Raven said angrily. "They just neglected to mention one tiny little detail."

"What's that?" Vaughn asked.

"That we already have a place with safe shops and restaurants and public spaces. It's called the town of Paradiso. And it's got a few things this mega-mall will never have—like a history and character, and a town green with real grass and trees!"

Raven's voice grew loud, and she could feel herself losing control. "And what's more, no one has to spend zillions of dollars pouring cement over our most important stretch of land!" she added.

"Hey, hey," Vaughn said softly, reaching out and giving a gentle tug on her long braid. "You don't have to convince *me*."

"But I have to convince *your* father," Raven blurted, her voice still angry. She saw Vaughn's face sag, and she instantly regretted her words. "Wow, listen to me," she said quietly. "I didn't mean that." Vaughn's body next to her was tight and stiff. "I'm sorry."

Vaughn nodded, but he didn't look at her. "Raven, I don't believe in what my dad's doing any more than you do. I'm trying to stop him. But it's not so easy on me. You know, a few nights ago Dad and I had another fight at dinner, and my mother left the table in tears." Vaughn was quiet for a moment. A tense quiet. The school lawn was filled with people, but their voices sounded far away. Then Vaughn said, "I like to think I have your support, at least."

Raven reached a tentative hand toward him. He took it in his. "You do," she said.

"Then you have mine," he answered.

"I know." Raven folded the ad in half and tucked it back in Vaughn's bag. "I didn't mean to take it out on you. But what they wrote—it's like saying that by trying to stop the mall, I'm partially to blame for April's death."

Raven had a sudden picture of April walking across the grassy lawn. The sun shone in her hair, and her jeans and blouse followed her curves as she moved. Raven had been reminded of that famous painting of a beautiful woman with long, wavy, flowing hair standing on half a scallop shell—an old Italian painting, she thought. April had that natural kind of beauty—something that came from inside. And now she was gone. Forever. And her killer was still out there.

"You know, sometimes I think all the energy I'm putting into the petition and the letter writing and everything is partly a way to avoid thinking about her too much," Raven said to Vaughn.

"At least you've got somewhere good to put the energy," Vaughn said. "April would approve."

"Yeah. We know April was on our side, don't we?" Raven said.

"Of course we do." Vaughn looked at her, and a smile played on his lips again. "You look nice to-day," he said. "Great skirt." It was the short, pleated plaid one.

"Brilliant with a needle and thread," Vaughn said. "In addition to everything else." He brought her hand to his lips and kissed her fingers, one by one.

But Raven still felt anxiety pumping through her. "Vaughn, what if they win? I mean, you and I know building a mall isn't going to stop April's killer from striking again. But people are so upset. Maybe they're willing to believe anything that'll make them feel better."

Vaughn put his hands on her shoulders and began to massage her back. His fingers were strong, working away the knots of tension. "Don't think that way," he said. "Senator Miller's doing his best to stall that bill that would let them rezone for the mall. And in the meantime, we're going to get the signatures of half the town of Paradiso."

"I know," Raven said. "Mmm. Yeah, right there. That's the spot. Just under my right shoulder blade." She leaned all her weight into his hands. "It's going to take more than just signatures. That'll hold them off for a while, but they'll just keep trying again and again, until they win. Unless we can get the scrublands official status as a wildlife sanctuary."

"What about that bird Winston was out photographing?"

"I sent the pictures to Senator Miller. He's got one of his assistants researching it. But Preston

Powell said he thought it was just a weird-looking robin."

Vaughn followed the muscles on either side of her back with his fingers. "Preston Powell? That dorky little kid who hangs out with your little brother?"

"Major authority on the bird and bug world," Raven said.

"Look, Raven, you're doing everything you can. We just have to think positive." Vaughn wrapped his arms around her. "Show my dad and Cal Pinkerton that they can't buy away people's convictions."

Raven thought of the hundred-dollar bill Calvin Pinkerton had given her the other day. It practically had *Ticket to Stanford* written all over it. She'd been trying hard to forget about it, but it kept pushing its way into her thoughts. It seemed as if the fight against the mall was going to get awfully dirty. It would be so easy to back off. Stanford was just waiting for her to tell them she was coming in September.

Raven was ashamed of her own thoughts. She buried herself in Vaughn's hug, feeling her face grow warm. "You—you really think it's worth all the fighting?" she asked him.

"Absolutely," Vaughn said.

Raven was glad to hear that his voice was sure

enough for both of them. She looked up at him and touched her fingertips to his mouth, tracing his lips. He cradled her face in his hands, leaning toward her. They met in a long, sweet, deep kiss. And another . . .

CHAPTER 18

A high-pitched, bloodcurdling scream echoed down the corridor. Hope froze, a vision of April's lifeless arm filling her mind. My God, no! It's happening again! she thought.

A second later the scream was followed by a loud, raucous laugh, a boy's laugh. Then a shrill, shaky girl's voice. "You scared me half to death!" she yelled. "What in the world is your problem?"

Hope rounded the corner to see Eddie Hagenspitzel grinning like an empty-headed jack-o'-lantern at a tiny girl with pale blond hair and freckles.

"You moron!" the girl yelled. "Were you just waiting behind those lockers to see who you could jump out at and terrify?"

"Just trying to get your attention," Eddie said.

"Hey! Don't storm off like that. It was just a joke. Katrina, wait!"

As the girl brushed past her, Eddie noticed Hope and gave a big shrug. "I've had chemistry class with her all year, and she never even looks at me," he said.

Hope could still feel her heart beating too fast. "Eddie, haven't you ever heard of calling a girl to get the homework assignment, or complimenting her on her shoes, or just going up to her and saying hello, like a normal person?"

Eddie pouted. "I was only trying to be funny."

"Well, you scared me half to death too," Hope said. She thought about the warning on the computer screen.

Eddie hung his big head and stood there, huge and chastened. "Maybe next time you see her, you should apologize. At least that'll give you an excuse to talk to her again," Hope said. "And in the meantime, take a break from terrorizing people in the hallways," she added as she walked away. Eddie really could be pretty funny, but sometimes he didn't know where to draw the line.

As Hope made her way toward the school's main exit, she felt the weight of Spike's things in her backpack. And the weight of having betrayed his secret—his and April's. She passed a group of junior girls standing in a little circle around the water fountain.

"Well, I heard that it was that gorgeous art teacher," she heard one of them say.

"Mr. Woolery?" one of her friends asked. "Boy, I wouldn't mind a date with him either."

"Nah, he's not the one," a third girl said. "Everyone knew she was going around with that motorcycle guy."

Hope couldn't stick around to hear any more. She knew the rumors weren't really her fault. The word about April's pregnancy would have gotten around no matter what. But how was Spike going to take it? April's note to him was deep in her pocket. Hope felt a bone-chilling fear. If you believed the talk at school today, Spike was number one on Paradiso's most wanted list. Mr. Woolery and Jess were running a close second and third.

Hope sighed, threading her way through the crowded hall and steering a wide berth around Bubba Dole. Psycho. Now there was a guy you'd think would be a suspect. But Spike and Jess? And April's favorite teacher?

Hope pushed open the door to the school and shuddered. It was as if April's death had been just the beginning of an evil spell. Now, under the beautiful, sunny Paradiso sky, the spell was really taking hold, and people were beginning to wonder how well they actually knew one another. Behind every tree in blossom lurked a murder suspect.

Hope crossed the gently sloping lawn of the school. She thought about the message on the computer terminal. And about the long, deserted walk to Spike's house. She was afraid it might be a mistake to go out there. A fatal mistake.

"Hope! Hey, Hope, wait up!"

Jess! Hope recognized the voice before she even turned around. He jogged to catch up to her, his reddish-blond hair wet from swimming, faint goggle marks still visible around his deep blue eyes. Hope felt the evil spell blow away on the gentle afternoon breeze. She knew she had a lovesick smile plastered to her face, but she couldn't help it.

"Hi! I haven't seen you all day," Jess said. His face was slightly flushed from running. It made him look even more handsome.

"Yeah, well, I've kind of been hiding," Hope explained. "Too many rumors, you know?"

"Tell me about it!" Jess shook his head. "I feel like I've got the first twentieth-century case of the bubonic plague. I bet I could clear out the cafeteria in about five minutes."

Hope bit her lip. She remembered how patient Jess had been in the garage, how gentle his fingers had felt on her face when he'd said good-bye in town. "I don't believe a word of it," she assured him.

He smiled. "Thanks, Hope. So. Where're you off to?"

Hope felt the books and sneakers in her bag. She had a feeling Jess would understand. "Spike's," she said. "I guess."

Jess nodded. "Now I see why he hasn't been around. Poor guy." He shook his head. "You knew, didn't you?"

"Yeah," Hope confirmed. "I promised I wouldn't say anything—for April's sake as much as Spike's. But now I'm afraid he's going to assume all the talk is my fault."

"You want me to come with you?" Jess asked. "It might not be the greatest idea for you to walk all the way out there by yourself anyway."

Good solution, Hope thought, again picturing the note on her computer. It *would* feel safer with Jess. Besides, she would have driven with Jess to the end of the world. "That'd be great," she said. "I mean, if you don't mind."

"Mind? I've been looking for you." Jess looked deep into her eyes. Hope felt out of breath, as if she were the one who had been running. "Come on," he said softly. "My car's in the lot."

A few minutes later, Hope was seated next to him in the GTO. As he pulled out of the student parking lot, she rolled down the window to let in the peach blossom breeze.

"It really helps to know you're on my side," Jess said, turning onto Old Town Road. "Today at school . . . Man, it was rough."

"I'm glad you caught up with me too," Hope said. Let people talk. In the middle of the most painful and difficult time in her life, Hope felt an oasis of pure happiness as she sat next to Jess Gardner. A few days ago, she hadn't thought it was possible. A few days ago, Jess had been an unapproachable dream.

As a large cloud passed in front of the sun, Hope felt a sudden chill. *An unapproachable dream.* So why was it that Jess seemed suddenly to be there every time she turned around? Why would he get interested in her like this, anyway? He was one of the most popular guys at school. Or he had been, until a couple of hours ago when the rumors started getting out of hand. Now there was probably an awful lot of people who would think Hope was out of her mind to be riding around with Jess.

Jess steered onto the pitted, narrow road that led to Spike's. "Hope? You okay?"

"Ah, yeah," Hope said. She tried to shake the ugly thoughts out of her head, but in her mind, she heard Sheriff Rodriguez's voice. *You might like Jess Gardner. But you can't rule out anyone.* What if it wasn't Spike she had to be nervous about visiting? What if the person she had to watch out for was sitting right beside her?

New questions tumbled through her mind. Why had Jess been looking for her after school? Was it for the express purpose of getting her into his car—alone? Had Jess just coincidentally been there when she'd found April's body? What if he'd been waiting to see her discover it? Hope hadn't even asked him if he really was driving around with April the night of the murder. The trees and sky outside her window rolled by in a blur, taking her farther and farther from town.

Stop! Hope told herself. This was crazy. The rumors, the fear, the note on her computer—they were all getting to her. Jess was her friend. Jess was one of the nicest guys she'd ever met. At least she thought he was. And that note on the computer—Jess wouldn't even have known how to leave it. Unless he knew more about computers than he'd told Hope he did.

She studied him as he followed the road. His nose curved down slightly in profile. His lips were full, his chin strong. He wore a navy blue sweatshirt. *Oh, God!* Hope remembered the flash of blue she'd seen disappearing down the hall after she'd gotten the warning message on the school computer. On Jess's cheek—was that a scratch Hope hadn't noticed before? One that had been made number of days ago and was almost—

BOOM! An explosion rocked the car, and it swerved wildly toward the trees at the edge of the road. Hope's own scream rang in her ears.

Jess struggled for control of the steering wheel. The car spun around nearly full circle before squealing to a stop. He instantly looked over at Hope. "Are you all right?"

Hope gulped in huge, frightened breaths. "Are you trying to get us killed?"

"We must have blown a tire," Jess said. He steered the car back in the right direction and eased the car off to the side of the road. Hope felt the thump, thump, thump of the blown-out tire. Jess turned off the ignition and let himself out of the car. Hope watched him go around to inspect the right rear tire. Her heart pounded in her ears.

"Yup," he called. "Big hole right through it."

Hope got out. Her legs were shaky. The sun spilled through the trees onto the car in dappled patterns of light and dark. Birds chirped overhead. There was no sign of another human being anywhere. They were all alone.

"Well, lesson number one, spark plugs," Jess said easily. "Lesson number two, how to change a flat tire. First, we get out the jack and the spare."

Hope watched Jess fit his key into the trunk

hood and lift it open. She gasped. There it was! The rope! The nylon rope that Penny had said she sold him. Hope swallowed a frightened cry.

Jess pushed the rope over to one side and began fishing around for what he needed. Hope was trembling as he took out the jack and a long, black metal bar. He unbolted the spare tire from the bottom of the trunk.

Hope pointed to the bar with a shaking finger. "What's that?" Her words came out in a whisper.

"Crowbar," Jess said.

"What's it for?"

"You'll see . . ."

Hope wanted to scream. She wanted to run.

"Hey, you're not nervous about changing a tire, are you?" Jess asked. "You'll do fine." He picked up the crowbar in one hand—the blunt, heavy steel bar—and took her arm in the other. He led her around to the punctured tire. "See it? See how the tire tread is all shredded right here?" He squatted down next to the wheel, lightly tugging Hope's arm.

She bent down on one knee to look at the blowout. She pretended to inspect the hole. Her mind was reeling, and her vision was blurry with terror. Suddenly she felt Jess release his grasp on her arm.

And then he was towering over her—the crowbar swinging in his hand.

CHAPTER 19

It wasn't supposed to be this way. Kiki dove into her pool and felt herself plunging down, down, down. High school wasn't supposed to end like this. She pulled through the water, feeling its weight on top of her as she slowly made her way to the surface. She burst through and took a deep breath of air. The late afternoon sun glinted off the water. Perfect, blue sky, Paradiso sun. It had been sunny every single day but one since April's murder. Somehow, Kiki felt it was wrong, as if it should have been rainy and gray all the time—weather more appropriate for a state of mourning.

She swam to the end of the pool with long, easy strokes, then did a flip-turn off the side and began swimming back. Senior year was supposed to end with a celebration, with high spirits and good friends. It was supposed to be a time to relax, before college. It should have been one of the best times of Kiki's life.

But all Kiki felt now was confusion. She wanted to swim as far away from Paradiso as she could. Away from her sadness, away from her fear, away from all her mixed-up emotions.

Kiki did another lap, swimming extra hard, as if that might get her somewhere farther away than the deep end of the De Santises' pool. If she and Lacey hadn't been fighting, she would at least have had some company. Lacey probably would have been stretched out on one of the deck chairs, pushing down the straps on her bikini top so that she wouldn't get a tan line and sipping an iced tea with lemon. "Save the calories for the cookies, babe," Lacey always said. She and Kiki would have moved the stereo speakers in the De Santises' living room so that they faced the pool area, and they would be blasting away the afternoon with some excellent tunes.

Kiki grabbed the edge of the pool and paused for a moment. Lacey would have known what she should do about Bobby, too. Of all the possible times to be feuding with your best friend, this one had to be the worst. Kiki thought about drying off and giving Lacey a call. But what would she say? "I'm ready to accept your apology, Lacey"?

Kiki plunged below the water's surface and swam

the next lap underwater. She started on her trip back without coming up. Finally, when her lungs felt as if they were going to burst, she swam up, swallowing air as soon as her head was out of the water. She opened her eyes. Looming over her, at the edge of the pool, was a figure draped in black.

Kiki gasped, blinking the stinging chlorinated water out of her eyes. The figure came into focus. "Mrs. Pinkerton!"

Lacey's mother was dressed head to toe in loose, gauzy black slacks and a matching top, a black silk scarf wrapped around her head, and her infamous sunglasses. She stood there like some sort of reverse ghost. Kiki swam over to her and looked up. "I was scared for a moment," she said with a little giggle.

Darla Pinkerton didn't say a word. Kiki felt the giggle die. "Um, my mom's not home right now, Mrs. Pinkerton."

"I didn't come here to talk to your mother, Kiki." Mrs. Pinkerton's voice was low and dark, a gathering thunderstorm.

Kiki felt a chill. She climbed out of the pool and, under Darla Pinkerton's stare, wrapped herself in her towel.

"They're rescheduling the Peach Blossom contest," Mrs. Pinkerton said.

Kiki nodded. She already knew she wasn't going to like this conversation.

190

"My daughter is sure to win. Just like I won when I was her age."

Under her damp towel, Kiki shuddered. How convenient for the Pinkertons that the real Queen of this year's Peach Blossom Festival was dead.

"Of course, it's every girl's dream to wear the crown," Lacey's mother continued, her eyes hidden behind the dark glasses, "but imagine your disappointment when the Queen is announced. Imagine all the people watching you struggle to keep a smile on your face as someone else's name is called."

Kiki sank to the edge of a lounge chair. Like mother, like daughter. Any desire she'd had to make up with Lacey vanished.

"You might want to save yourself the humiliation of losing," Darla Pinkerton said. She followed Kiki to the chair and hovered over her.

Kiki swallowed and gathered her courage. "Mrs. Pinkerton, I think I'll let the committee decide who wins." Lacey must have put her mother up to this. She had to have. Or was Darla Pinkerton so desperate on her own?

"If I were you, I'd consider it very carefully. It might be a much smarter idea to drop out." Darla Pinkerton turned and walked away slowly. Over her shoulder she trailed one more menacing sentence. "If you know what's good for you. . . ."

CHAPTER 20

The sun was low and swollen. The light hit the tall grass from a sharp angle, coloring one side with deep purple shadows. Raven felt a breeze picking up, blowing across the fields and bending the tree branches back and forth in a slow dance. The scrublands had an eerie kind of beauty in the late afternoon.

Raven tried to imagine the scrublands paved over, a mass of glass and steel and concrete, surrounded by a mile-square parking lot. Where would she go to collect her thoughts, or when she needed privacy, or was upset, or just wanted to listen to the wind? To the plastic and the fluorescent lights of King Chicken or the Shoe Rack in the Greenway Mall?

Raven spread her arms out, spinning, her face up to the vast, darkening sky. She breathed in sweet grass and pungent earth and fresh air. Here, she felt like a part of nature—one tiny part, in a huge and powerful whole that was beyond any single person or problem. Here, Raven surrendered her worries to the monstrous and miraculous forces of the earth.

At home, her mother lay in bed, sick, and no one could figure out why. Her brothers and sisters strained the little house behind the café to its walls, bunking four in the boys' room and three in the girls'. At the café, customers talked in hushed tones about tragedy and murder. But here, that world faded. At least for a while. Here, Raven could shut it all out.

She spun until she grew dizzy, falling right down into the grass. She lay on her back and stared up at the sky, watching an occasional wispy cloud drift past. Let Calvin Pinkerton toss hundred-dollar bills and big promises around. She wasn't going to back off. This land was too important.

She closed her eyes, willing the tension of the horrible, frightening days since April's death to drain away. The sun caressed one side of her face, breeze and shadow the other. Raven felt herself drifting into the twilight state between wakefulness and sleep. Her breath was deep and relaxed, her thoughts loose. She imagined Vaughn's arms around her. She felt his body next to hers. The grass swayed. *Snap!* A twig cracked near her ear.

Raven bolted upright. A man stood in front of her, blocking out the sun. Fear gripped her throat. His face was darkened into a silhouette by the low sun behind his head. Raven raised her hands to ward him off. He stepped away, out of the path of light.

"Mr. Woolery!"

"Raven!" Mr. Woolery's voice was as shaky as hers. "What are you doing lying there like—like you were . . ." His sentence trailed off.

"What are *you* doing here?" Raven countered. She dropped her arms to her sides, but they were still trembling.

"I frightened you, didn't I?" he asked. "I'm sorry." He squatted down to face her. "I got scared too, when I saw you lying here."

Raven gave a short, nervous laugh. "I'm fine," she said. But her mind was filled with all the talk about Mr. Woolery, and with the story Kiki had told about him at the café before school.

"I needed to find some peace and quiet," Mr. Woolery said. "Sort out everything that's happened."

Raven nodded. "Me too." But her guard was still up. This was the same spot that Mr. Woolery had come to with April, just before her death. Had something happened here that only Mr. Woolery knew about? That April had known about before she'd been murdered? The bruise-colored shadows cast by the low sun suddenly seemed sinister and the birds' calls urgent, ominous.

Raven got to her feet. "Well, I'll let you be alone, Mr. Woolery." She was already backing away.

Mr. Woolery also stood up, his movie star features creasing in a look of pain. "Raven, I didn't mean to run you away," he said quietly. "I know this is a special place for you. It is for me too."

Raven felt a jolt of sympathy. Mr. Woolery had to know what people were saying. On the other hand, maybe there was something to the rumors. Maybe his sad expression was a mask. Maybe Mr. Woolery had a dark secret. "I—I was going to go anyway," Raven said. "Dinner shift at the café."

"I see," Mr. Woolery said. He didn't try to stop her. "Take care, Raven." He sounded so sincere. His brown eyes reflected a well of sadness, dug by loss and harsh talk. "Take care," he said again. Or was there a warning in his voice?

Raven said good-bye and began walking. She hated herself for thinking such terrible things about Mr. Woolery. He'd been April's favorite teacher. He was one of SCAM's biggest supporters among the Paradiso High staff. The buttons had been his idea, and he'd designed them himself. Raven touched the green and black SCAM button on her shirt. Perhaps running away from Mr. Woolery wasn't the answer. Perhaps she should stay and talk. He missed April too. They both might find some comfort in conversation.

Raven looked back over her shoulder at the art teacher. He had stooped back down again, as if he had discovered something on the ground. Raven watched as he reached down, his arm disappearing into the tall grass. He stood up and dropped something into his shirt pocket. Whatever it was gave off a wink as it was momentarily caught in the sun's rays.

Raven's fear took swift hold again. Had Mr. Woolery lost something when he'd been there with April? Something he couldn't risk someone else finding? Some sort of awful evidence? Was that the real reason he'd come there this afternoon?

One hand shielding his eyes from the sun, Mr. Woolery turned toward Raven and raised his other arm over his head. He motioned to her and called her name. The syllables were barely audible on the light breeze. She watched him start toward her, coming closer, closer . . .

Raven didn't stick around to see any more. She turned her back on Mr. Woolery again and walked more quickly. Then she ran.

CHAPTER 21

Next to Jess Gardner's empty car, the crowbar lay on the ground like a dead snake. Hope shuddered. She thought about the way it had glinted as Jess had swung it back and forth. She remembered the sour taste of fear rising in her throat. Had April felt the same thing, just before she'd been killed? For Hope it had been a false alarm—panic and imagination coming together in a moment of icy terror. For April it had been too real—the last moment she would ever experience.

Hope tried not to think about it as she paced up and down next to the car. But Jess had run off to get help, and she was alone and she was scared. She hadn't managed entirely to shake off the ominous feeling that had been growing inside her, and her thoughts about April took root in her fear. The birds sang frightening dusk sounds, and the trees loomed like giants at the edge of the road.

197

What was taking Jess so long? He'd discovered something wrong with the jack, and he'd gone ahead to Spike's to borrow some tools. "Sit tight," he'd told Hope. "I'll be back in a flash." But he'd left more than fifteen minutes ago. She felt awful for thinking those ugly things about Jess. But April's murder was like a foul rain, watering seeds of doubt and suspicion about the people you liked most. Even now, Hope felt a bud of wariness about Jess. A blown-out tire *and* a broken jack. It was almost as if he'd planned to leave her by herself on the side of the road.

Don't be silly, Hope Hubbard, she thought. Jess is the most terrific, best-looking boy in the—

"Ahhh!" Hope's cry split the twilight as something whizzed by her ear. A stone cracked the windshield behind her. Suddenly she was running, her heart pounding in her ears, horror racing through her body. Her legs seemed to move all by themselves. She took off into the trees, dodging bushes and fallen logs. She was running too hard to even turn around to glance behind her, too afraid to see Jess chasing after her. She pumped her long legs harder than she had known she could, running deeper and deeper into the woods. She swallowed huge, gasping breaths. Her lungs felt as if they might burst.

Keep going. Keep running, she told herself. It's

your only chance. She wove in and out of the trees. She kept running, bursting out of the dense underbrush and haphazard arrangement of trees in the woods and into a grassy orchard of peach trees in neat rows. She ran more easily on the cleared ground, vaguely aware of the soft carpet of peach blossom petals her sneakers crushed with each step.

As she sprinted between two rows of trees another flat stone whipped by her, ricocheting off the trunk of a tall tree. Then pain shot through Hope's entire body as a sharp rock tore her cheek. Hope stumbled and slammed into a huge root swelling out of the ground beneath her. She screamed in pain as she felt herself going down, falling, collapsing on the grass.

Hope reached up and touched her face. She looked at her hand. It was covered with dark red blood. Behind her, a twig snapped. She turned her head, weak with fear. Jess!

Instead of coming to finish her off, he ran along the edge of the woods. Way ahead of him, Hope could barely make out a shadowy figure in a hooded sweatshirt.

Hope struggled to sit. Jess was too far behind to catch up, but as the hooded figure vanished into the woods, he turned and followed. Hope could hear him crashing through the woods, then the sound died out. She sat on the ground, her ankle throbbing and her face on fire. Tears streamed onto her face, intensifying the pain, and Hope dropped back to the ground. Time froze. Maybe only a few moments passed. Maybe it was an hour. Finally, Jess stumbled back into the clearing—alone.

"Jess!" Hope called. Instinctively she raised a hand to cover the ugly, sticky mixture of tears and blood on her face. She got up slowly. The pain seemed to have spread through every fiber of her body. She wanted to hold on to something, to steady herself, but there was nothing . . .

Jess raced to meet her, his arms reaching out for her. "Hope, Hope! Are you all right? You could have been killed!"

She was in his arms. He held her as she trembled. She could feel him trembling too. "Oh, Jess, you saved me . . . you saved my life."

Jess released a long breath. "But he got away. I just couldn't catch up. And it's too dark in the woods to see."

"You could have gotten killed yourself," said Hope. She felt herself shaking even harder.

Jess stroked her hair. "It's okay. It's all right, Hope. We're both alive. We'll be okay. . . ."

Hope laid her head against Jess's chest. His heart beat loudly. "Jess, forgive me."

"Forgive you? For what?"

"Oh, Jess, I thought . . . that you . . . I can't

even say it." Jess was never going to want to talk to her again. She took a deep breath. "The rope in the back of the car. Everything everyone at school's saying. Getting chased . . . Oh, Jess, please don't hate me."

Jess took Hope's face in his hands and looked into her teary eyes. "You thought that I might want to hurt you? You thought I wanted to hurt April?"

Hope turned her face from him. She moved away. Her whole body was hot with shame. She couldn't talk. How could she not have trusted Jess?

"Hope, I've known April all my life," Jess said. "I mean, I knew her. She was my friend. I'm going to miss her. I do miss her."

Hope nodded, but she couldn't meet Jess's gaze. "I knew you weren't the one. I knew I shouldn't believe it. But then . . . I got scared. It's *my* fault. . . ."

In the deepening darkness, Jess shook his head. "Maybe it's my fault. I should've told you right away."

"Told me what?" Hope asked.

"About April. Giving her a ride," Jess began. "I did see her walking along the road, so I offered her a ride. She got in; she was nearly hysterical. She told me everything about Spike, and the rumor that Lacey was hitting on him, and she told me about the baby. Then she seemed really ashamed that she had told me, and she asked me to let her out. She never said where she was going. She said she wanted to be by herself. Said she had things to think about. I promised not to tell anyone about what she told me, or even that I had seen her. But now that everyone knows everything anyway, I don't think it can hurt her anymore."

"I'm sorry," Hope said, her face on fire with shame and regret. "I should have believed what I knew deep down."

"It's okay," Jess said. There was a moment of silence. Hope was suddenly aware of the soft, sweet smell of peach blossoms in the air. Jess took a step toward her and knelt by her side. Then they were in each other's arms.

Jess kissed the top of her head. Pale peach blossoms floated down on them. The moon was a silvery shadow on the newly dark sky. Hope felt Jess's heart pounding next to hers. She took in his every feature, memorizing his face with her eyes. He was so close. Closer, closer. Their lips met. Hope melted into the kiss she'd dreamed about. A long, passionate kiss.

But in Paradiso, that did not mean you could live happily ever after. April's murderer was still free—and free to kill again.